The Wit and Wisdom
of an Old Muskrat Trapper:
Essays and Stories

By Ray M. Theuret

Edited by Bonnie Walker

The Wit and Wisdom of an Old Muskrat Trapper:

Essays and Stories

By Ray M. Theuret

Edited by Bonnie Walker

apprentice house

Baltimore, Maryland
www.apprenticehouse.com

Apprentice House is an imprint of Resonant Publishing

Those parties involved in this publication take
no responsibility for typographical errors
or misprints. Every effort was made
to ensure the accuracy of information
included in this book.

Project Manager: Elizabeth Didora
Assistant Editors: Michelle Betton and Katharine Dailey
Cover design by Bonnie Walker

First printing
10 9 8 7 6 5 4 3 2 1

ISBN: 978-1-933051-04-8

apprentice
house

Baltimore, Maryland
www.apprenticehouse.com

apprentice
house

Apprentice House is a non-profit activity of the Department of Communication at Loyola College in Maryland. The organization is an activity of an advanced elective in the journalism concentration, Book Publishing. When the class is not in session the publishing activities are carried forward by a co-curricular organization, The Apprentice House Book Publishing Club pursues publishing activities through Resonant Publishing, whose principal, Dr. Kevin Atticks, is a member of the Communication faculty. Apprentice House is an imprint of Resonant Publishing.

Apprentice House is just one of many experiential learning opportunities available to Loyola students in all our Communication disciplines: journalism, advertising, public relations, digital media, radio and television, and writing. Students are responsible for manuscript selection, editing, author contact, permissions, pricing, production, design, marketing and publicity. Those who complete the course and other students interested in working for Apprentice House can register for a follow-up Practicum in Book Publishing.

Student Editors (2004-05)

Cook Alciati '06	Lauren Galvin '05
Michael Barry '05	Marion Goodworth '05
Michelle Betton '05	Morgan Hillenbrand '05
Jeffrey Bradley '05	Michael Hilt '05
Kristen Cesiro '07	Patricia McNamara '06
Katharine Dailey '06	Lindsay Miller '05
Christine DeSanctis '05	Kathleen Nagle '05
Elizabeth Didora '05	Kerri Reilly '05
Michael Hilt '05	Erik Schmitz '07

Dedication

*This book is dedicated to the Bowie Senior Writers' Group
and its founders, Winoma and Art Ackerman,
whose members enriched the life of the author
of this book immeasurably; and
to the members of his much loved
Writers' Group at Lighthouse Point.*

Acknowledgements

Many thanks to all of the members of the Bowie Senior Writers' Group and the Lighthouse Point Writers' Group who nurtured the writings that appear in this collection. They were the audience and the inspiration. Lee Stoops deserves special recognition and thanks for the many hours spent reading these pieces and offering constructive suggestions and encouragement to the author. Also, thanks to Neil Potash one of the members of the Bowie Senior Writers' Group whose encouragement and appreciation meant a lot to Ray Theuret and who helped the editor locate some of the pieces that are included in this collection.

Table of Contents

Introduction

My father was Ray Morse Theuret. In April of 2004 he called me on the telephone from Pompano Beach, Florida to discuss a few of his last requests. He wanted to me to immediately go to a funeral home in Bowie and to make arrangements for his burial. He wanted a funeral with all the trimmings including a solid oak casket. He instructed me to go to a cemetery near Bowie and purchase a family plot. He gave me specific instructions for his memorial stone. I promised to do this immediately, as he requested, even though I insisted he would not be needed it for a long time. I reminded him that his cousin Ruth was 103 and that he was still a kid. "Nevertheless," he responded patiently, "do it so I don't need to worry about it anymore. If I don't need it for a while, well that's okay."

There was one more thing that he wanted me to do. His request was to gather up all of the essays and stories that he had written and to publish them and give copies to his friends in his two writers' groups, one in Bowie, Maryland and the other at Lighthouse Point in Pompano Beach, Florida. This collection is the result.

My father passed away at 7 a.m. on June 3, 2004 in the living room of his home in Bowie, Maryland with my mother and me at his bedside holding his hands. We had known this was going to happen for a few days, but nothing could prepare us for the finality of this event. He was completely at peace. In the moment before he took his last breath, he opened his eyes, looked at my mother and me, smiled, and moved his mouth as though trying to say something. Then he left his body.

An hour later the undertaker was there to take him to the funeral home, leaving my mother and me with instructions to be there at 11 a.m. to make arrangements for the viewing. We had already made all the other decisions that were needed, per his request in April. For the rest of that day and for the next four days, we were fully occupied with funeral plans, the viewing, and visitors from out of town. It was not until a few days later that we realized that he was really gone. My reliable, dependable, always

Here I am with my father at age 5, securely tucked under his protective arm.

there for me father had truly left us, not on a business trip or a golfing trip, but forever. At least his body was gone.

Reading through the essays and stories, editing them for publication, as he had asked me to do, I realized two things. First, my father knew that I especially would need a pretty substantial "to do" list for a while. Second, that he had left so much of himself behind. All of us who knew him, loved him. I was never aware of a single person who didn't like and respect my father. He had given much of himself to others all of his life and through this collection of his writing, he continues to share himself with his friends and family and future generations who may be able to read this collection.

One other thing I need to say about this collection is that these essays are in his words. My editing consisted of checking spelling, grammar, and punctuation, and selecting the pieces that are included here. Everything else came from the heart and soul of a man who liked to refer to himself as just an "Old Muskrat Trapper."

Bonnie Lee Theuret Walker
Rehoboth Beach, Delaware
July 10, 2004

Foreword

Memorial tribute delivered on June 7, 2004 by Reverend Richard Stetler, at St. Matthew's United Methodist Church, Bowie, Maryland

I clipped an article on diamonds some months ago that gave some very interesting information about how these minerals are formed. Most diamonds are 3 billion years old, but there are few younger ones, which are only 628 million years old. If you are wearing a diamond, the chances are good that your diamond is half as old as the earth. The majority of diamonds were formed 100 miles below the surface of the earth by heat and pressure, producing a crystal from carbon.

Lives that radiate a brilliance also come from responding to their environment with wholesome thoughts, nonjudgmental attitudes and a strong desire to bring to the surface all the treasures that God allowed to form within them at birth. The words "fear" and "defeat" were not part of Ray Theuret's vocabulary. He turned everything into a teacher, always learning, always growing, and always maturing in spirit. He became a human diamond with many marvelous facets packaged around a very unassuming, humble personality.

Ray came into the world on December 9, 1912 in Chapmansville, Pennsylvania. He was reared in a very theologically conservative denomination, The Church of God. Ray, however, never parked his mind at the door when he came to church. He was an excellent thinker. During his life he learned to take the grain his numerous churches had to offer and with a breath of kindness, he blew the chaff away. One of those grains was a gal named Alice whom he met in his youth group. Once the two of them held hands, they never looked back.

Ray and his twin brother Roy were inseparable. They fished, hunted and trapped muskrats. Their family was poor, but Ray knew that poverty never hurt anyone who had vision and a sense of adventure. Ray loved the challenges that life brought him. Each ripple that came his way allowed more and more of his skills to surface.

Ray and Alice married in 1938 and a year later Bonnie was born. It seemed that Ray was blessed with a pair of itchy feet. The family moved every year when Bonnie was in grade school. Alice was always packing and unpacking. They were always moving to the next job.

Ray had only a high school diploma, but studied constantly for his CPA exam. His love of numbers fueled his passion. Bonnie was nine when he landed that CPA certificate and he proudly hung it on the wall in the front hallway where everyone entering the house could see it. Aside from his capturing Alice and having Bonnie and his son Richard, becoming a CPA was one of his proudest accomplishments.

Ray was constantly on the move. He loved living out of a suitcase. He thrived on his numerous travels. He went to Europe many times, Japan, Okinawa, Hong Kong, Korea, and numerous other countries. When his granddaughter, April was born, Ray managed to engineer a trip to audit some books in Frankfurt, Germany where Bonnie was living. Ray suggested the name April because of how his mind worked. He had an Aunt May and a sister-in-law named June. An "April" was needed in order to balance the audit on the family tree.

Ray's life was successful because he never took himself too seriously. He treated most people as equals. He listened more than he talked. He never forgot important details. He learned to live the faith he had grown to love. A person could count on Ray being there without complaint or the slightest hint of being inconvenienced. When you were with him, you were the only pebble on his beach. He absolutely loved every member of his family, Ola, his sister who is here today, his nephew Lavern Tingley who was like a second son who is also here.

Ray loved competition. He taught his son-in-law Bill Knott, how to play golf and could not stand it when his prized pupil began to beat him. He would quietly tell intimates that he experienced three holes in one during his golfing career.

The youthful adventurer in Ray never grew up. In his 80s he went to Alaska with family for a week of fishing, hunting, and partying. When he came home, he slept for three days. He counted as one of the highlights of his life a fishing trip he took with his son Richard in Minnesota where his best friend from childhood, Walt Fuhrman lived.

Ray possessed the same spirit as Mark Twain who wrote the tales of Tom Sawyer and Huck Finn and wrote a book about his own childhood adventures titled *Franklin Park*. He also wrote a lengthy book entitled *The Life and Times of Ray Theuret*, a volume that is chuck full of information about those incredible years spent with a number of incredible people.

Ray's retirement years were filled with the knowledge that he accomplished most dreams he set out to achieve. He did it all while remaining faithful to the values he cherished. For the last 30 years he and Alice wintered in Pompano Beach, Florida. They spent their summers in Bowie, Maryland where they could be nearer their children, grandchildren, and great-grandchildren. While in Bowie, they were faithful attendees at St. Matthew's every Sunday they were able.

Recently, Ray had one last desire. He wanted to get home from Florida so that he could leave his body while at home in Bowie. He began orchestrating his memorial service many months ago. Even his last wish was accomplished.

I'm sure he heard the voice of God say, "Ray, well done my good and faithful servant. You have been faithful over so few things, I will make you ruler over much. Enter into the gates of my Kingdom." Ray did just that.

Part One: *Essays*

The twins: Roy and Ray as infants. The bond between them was ever present throughout their lives.

Begat

This essay, written for his writer's group, was first delivered in 1997.

One of the most easily recognized as well as the most intriguing words in the Bible is the word "begat." For example, Adam begat Seth, Seth begat Enosh, Enosh begat Kenan, and so on. As far as I personally know, this verb is not used elsewhere in literature. And in the Bible it is used only in the King James Version, which written during the age of Shakespeare, has a musical and poetical quality that later versions lack. The word "begat" has a sexual connotation, and this may be the reason that the writers of the Revised Standard Version of the Bible, and other versions, changed "begat" to "he was the father of." In my opinion, something was lost in these revised translations. The word "begat" was not used in any Catholic versions of the Bible.

When we see or here the word "begat" we know of a certainty that it is biblical. Offhand, I can think of no other word for which this can be said. The word "begat" denotes a deliberate effort to procreate while "he was the father of" can and in this day often is purely unintentional.

God told Adam and Eve to be fruitful and multiply and fill the earth. Man has followed this commandment so faithfully over the millenniums since the creation that today there are four or more billion of us. If we keep on begatting at our present rate, by the twenty-second century, the number of people on earth will exceed the number of stars in the sky, a promise God made to Abraham. Of interest to feminists, it is noted, that in only rare instances is the female part in the "begats" mentioned by name.

When I wrote my autobiography, I could have simplified the part that describes my ancestral background if I had followed the order that is given to us in the King James Version of the Old Testament. Using such a format I would have started with my great-grandfather, Joseph Point Theuret. Joseph Point begatted six children while he still lived in France of which my Grandfather Augustus was number six, the last one begatted in France. After he migrated to America, Joseph Point kept on begatting and had five more children. I do not know who begatted Joseph Point. I hope it was somebody by the name of Theuret and not some soldier passing through Northeastern France on his way to a Napoleonic battle. All of Joseph Point's begattings, as far as I know, were done with the help of his one wife, Elizabeth Kareskind. Joseph Point lived to the age of ninety-five so all this begatting doesn't seem to have harmed him. I suspect, although I do not know this for a fact, that Joseph Point's principal part in raising such a large family was limited to the begetting, and it was Elizabeth who had the burden of bringing up the children.

My Grandfather Augustus married Hannah Hays. Hannah was the first of thirteen children begatted by John Hays with the aid of his wife Sarah. Great-grandfather John is the champion begatter in my father's ancestry as far as I know. However, on my mother's side of my ancestry there is a tradition that one of her ancestors, during the War of Independence and the years that followed, begatted twenty children. Tradition also says that he had at least two wives and probably more.

In biblical times, and in our own times, up to the 20th Century, large families were much to be desired. In biblical times children were needed to help work the land, to herd the sheep and goats, and to provide armies for protection from numerous warlike neighbors. Prior to the 20th Century large families were also desirable in the United States. The majority of Americans lived on small farms. Before the development of present day farm machinery all work was done by hand with the exception of plowing where the use of oxen or a horse was common. Planting was done by hand one seed at a time. When a field of corn was planted, for example, the more children in the family to help the better. Even a little tot could poke a hole in the ground with a stick, drop a seed into the hole and stomp it down. This method of planting continues in the Far East. When it comes time to plant the rice seedlings, the whole family can be seen wading in the dirty water and thrusting the seedlings into the ground beneath the water.

Another factor in the need for a large birthrate in ancient times and in this country up to the 20th Century was the number of children who died in infancy. In the Bible little or no mention is made of the death of infants. But such deaths must have been as common as in this country before the development of modern medicine.

With the development of modern farm machinery, with which one man can farm more land than ten or more large families could in the past, there is no need to have large families to grow our food. Almost all children born today grow into adults due to modern medicine. There is no need to have eight children today so that four will survive. The sexual instinct, however, still remains in mankind although the need for this instinct has been reduced. This instinct is used today for largely recreational purposes not for procreation as connoted by the word "begat."

Out Of Place

This essay was written and delivered to his writers' group in 1997 or 1998.

I was hired by the U. S. Army as a civilian accountant in 1941. Although I had readily passed the civil service test for the position, I had never held an accounting position up to that time. During the prior 10 years, since graduation from high school in 1931, my work experience consisted of 7 years with the telephone company as an addressograph clerk and 3 years at a zipper factory as an inspector. It was the time of the Great Depression and during this period I was happy to have any job at all.

During the first three years that I worked for the Army, I was in a subordinate position and did not have to deal personally with high officials either in the government or with the companies with whom the Army did business. This all changed in early 1944 when I was promoted to a position of senior accountant.

One of the first assignments that I received from my boss, Major Palmer, after my promotion was to go to New York City to the offices of Haskins and Sells, a national firm of Certified Public Accountants. I was to give advice to these accountants and their client Reynolds Metal Corporation as to how to submit claims against the Army on terminated contracts. Although Reynolds Metal was a well-known producer of aluminum, I had never heard of them at the time.

On arrival at Haskins and Sells I was ushered into the board room. In this large luxurious room was a long mahogany table with leather-covered chairs along the sides to match. Expensive carpeting covered the floor and beautiful paintings hung on the walls. There was a chair at the head of the table at which I was placed. I had never been in such a room before. In a few minutes the treasurer and the comptroller of Reynolds Metal along with a couple of assistants came into the room and introduced themselves. Two partners of Haskins and Sells and several senior accountants followed them closely.

I was by far the least qualified person in the room. It was my responsibility, however, to lead the meeting and to give advice where needed. I thought to myself, "What is an old muskrat trapper like me doing here." I felt like Willy Miranda, a notorious poor hitter, would have felt if sent in to bat for Mickey Mantle.

As soon as I opened the meeting, the company officials and the accountants took over. I hardly got a word in edgewise. The few words I did get in were generally something like, "Yes, that sounds all right." or "Fine." or "OK." I adhered to the old saying, "Better to keep your mouth shut and be thought a fool than to open it and remove all doubt."

In spite of my lack of real participation, or perhaps because of it, the meeting was a complete success. The Reynolds Metal officials and the Haskins and Sells CPAs discussed the problem for about thirty minutes and came to a decision among themselves as to what should be done. My advice was seldom, if ever, asked as I recall, and I volunteered nothing. As the meeting adjourned, the company officials and the accounting firm partners thanked me for being so much help to them.

As the years went by and my experience increased, I got used to meetings like the foregoing. By the time I became a CPA myself, I no longer felt that CPAs or high corporation officials were semi-gods as I thought at the time of my meeting with Haskins and Sells and Reynolds Metal in 1944.

Ramblings

This essay was delivered to his writer's group in Bowie, Maryland on October 20, 1997.

When I retired from the government in 1972, I considered that the main part of my life was over and that during the years to follow I would have to sustain myself on my memories of the past sixty years and the friends made during those years. I had had an interesting life, but I thought the interesting part was over. I expected to spend the years remaining to me in leisure and comfort and little else. How wrong I was. My life was far from over.

During the twenty-five years since I retired I have taken on avocations that I had no time for before I retired and gained many friends that have become as important to me as the friends I had gained over my first sixty years. It is true that many of my old friends have passed on and many of my new friends as well. Each one, old or new, has enriched my life and I hope that at least in some small measure I enriched theirs also. I have found that you are never too old to make new friends. In making new friends I take care not to lose the friends I have gained in the past. Once you have made friends never let them go. Keep them, whatever it takes, for they are true treasures of life.

Three years before I retired, my wife Alice and I, while visiting Alice's sister and brother-in-law, Marie and Earl Strict in Florida, decided to buy a condominium apartment at Seahaven in Pompano Beach, Florida as a retirement home. The apartment, one of 338 units, was under construction at the time. When it was finished in 1970, we rented it to a couple from Maryland, Harold and Georgia Hayes. They had lived not far from us in Maryland, but we had not previously known them. Upon retirement they had sold their home in Maryland with the intention of moving to Florida on a permanent basis. We became good friends. They stayed in our apartment only a year, and then decided they wanted to return to Maryland to live. When they returned to Maryland, we continued our friendship. They have since passed on but the good memories remain.

We moved to Florida in July 1972. We had stayed in our apartment several times on vacation, both before and after we rented the apartment to the Hayes. We had become acquainted with a few of the people who lived in Seahaven during these stays. Consequently when we moved to Seahaven in July 1972, we were not complete strangers to several of the condominium residents. During our first vacation to Seahaven, we bought enough furniture to survive, a bed to sleep in, a couple of chairs to sit on, a kitchen table to eat on and a lamp or two, but not much more. Rugs came with the apartment. I suppose that if we were to do this today one of the first things we would buy is a television. But television in 1970 wasn't quite as necessary to us as it is today. It was not important to us, especially when we were on vacation. However, after we moved to Florida and finished furnishing the apartment, one of the first things we bought was a television. During the next two years we returned several times to our home in Maryland. In 1974 we sold that home and more or less committed ourselves to Florida.

The residents of Seahaven were predominately retired business or professional people. Most had been in some kind of business for themselves or had held important positions in larger businesses. There were several retired doctors, lawyers, engineers and Certified Public Accountants among the residents. Several, like myself, had recently retired from government positions, both

Federal and State. It was surprising, at least to me, how easy it was to get acquainted with the other residents of Seahaven and how quickly we made friends. Over the passing years many of these friends have become as important to us as the old friends we made in the years before we moved to Florida. Most of the people in the condominium had, like us, moved away from relatives and friends and from places where they had lived a lifetime. Most of them were as anxious as we were, to make new friends. Within a year I was on the Seahaven Board of Directors and was treasurer of the condominium.

We met people at the pool and at condominium parties. That fall a bowling league was started which we joined and became acquainted with more people. Alice joined the ladies exercise class and made several more acquaintances. We kept our close relationship with Alice's sister and brother-in-law, Marie and Earl Strict. They had a wide circle of friends who had moved to Southern Florida from their hometown of Erie, Pennsylvania. We became friends, in some cases close friends, with them also.

Soon after we moved to Florida I started to play golf with my brother-in-law Earl at a Par 3 course in Ft. Lauderdale. Earl and I played with a man, Otto Sobota, who had recently retired and moved to Florida from Maryland. Alice had worked with his wife. I played very poorly at first. In fact Otto soon told me that I would have to play better if I was going to play with him and Earl. Earl and Otto had played golf most of their adult lives. Well, I did improve. Within a year or two I had improved to the extent that neither Earl nor Otto were competitive with me.

With the improvement in my golf skills I decided to join the Pompano Beach Country Club. The Pompano Beach Country Club has two regular size golf courses. At the bowling alley I had learned there were several golf foursomes in Seahaven who played at the Pompano Beach Country Club on a regular basis. The golfers of Seahaven formed foursomes based on skill, which is normal in golf. At first, based on my own skill, I played with the poorer golfers in Seahaven. Once in a while I would get to play with some of the better golfers. When I returned to my regular foursome I would receive comments such as, "I see you played with the Big Boys last week." Eventually I became skilled enough so that I played with the "Big Boys" on a regular basis.

I continued, on a weekly basis, to play golf with my brother-in-law Earl at his Par 3 course. Otto had decided to play golf at another Par 3 golf course nearer his home. Whenever Earl wanted to I would bring him to the Pompano Beach Country Club. The courses were too long for him. He was in his eighties at the time. I kept score and I made sure he need not be shamed by his score.

A couple years after I started to play golf at the Pompano Beach Country Club, Alice decided she would like to play golf, also. Three

The golfers. In retirement Ray Theuret achieves his secret life goal, to be a full time professional athlete.

other women, at the condominium, were of a like mind. They played at first at a pitch and put course and then, after becoming consistently able to hit the ball, to a Par 3 course. After several months they decided to play the "big" courses of the Pompano Beach Country Club. They went to the Pro for a group lesson, but he gave them just one lesson. He recommended that they just go out on the course and enjoy themselves and not take any more lessons. Two of Alice's foursome are now gone but Alice still plays with the lady that remains.

We joined a church where we were acquainted with a family we had known back in Erie, Pennsylvania in 1940. We attended this church on a regular basis and became acquainted with most of the members. We became intimate only with the family we knew from Erie and with two men who were golfers, one of whom has since died. A church is a good place to make friends. But to do so you should involve yourself in the programs of the church. We did not do this. With the exception of attending Christmas parties, our involvement in church affairs was generally limited to giving it financial support and attending Sunday morning services. But nevertheless we did become acquainted with a lot of nice people who we enjoyed seeing and visiting with on Sunday mornings.

The men who became my best friends were the golfers. Eventually I had a foursome who I played with on a regular basis. In addition to golf, we, together with the other golfers in Seahaven, socialized at parties, going out to restaurants, and taking golf vacations to other locations in Florida. Our wives always participated in these affairs and in these trips. Some of the golfers, including myself, went north in the summertime. We visited back and forth during the summer and played golf together. Our trips to visit each other were vacations from the doldrums of summer.

During the early period of my retirement I did little writing. I did work spasmodically on my memoirs, but I made little progress. In 1979, I took a trip to Alaska and I wrote a detailed story of this most pleasurable trip. I read excerpts from the story at a party to the relatives I was visiting in Alaska and their friends. It was well received. This experience, later on, encouraged me to try my hand at writing on other subjects. However, for several years I did little writing except to work once in a while on my autobiography.

In 1984 I decided to try to write a story that had been in my mind for several years. I called it "Chicken Soup." After I had finished the story my daughter, Bonnie, put the story on her computer and at the same time correcting my numerous misspellings and punctuating it so that it read smoothly. My relatives and friends who read "Chicken Soup" enjoyed its humor and this encouraged me to try my hand at other short stories. I eventually ended with twelve stories which I have, with the aid of my daughter, published in a private printing for my relatives and friends. While I was writing my short stories, I decided to write a history of my involvement in the U. S. Any Audit Agency where I worked for nineteen years and from where I retired. I had this book privately printed, also. I gave copies to my friends in the Agency, mostly retired. The demand was so great that I had to have it reprinted. My second printing included pictures. My first printing had contained none. My experience was limited but I was learning.

While I was writing my short stories and Army Audit Agency memoirs, I worked occasionally on my autobiography. I made some progress. My writings were handwritten on long yellow pads. When I came north to Maryland from Florida in 1992, I thought about my age, seventy-nine, and decided that if I was ever to get it finished I had better get working on it. I finished drafting my story on my long yellow pads. I worked that summer for two and a half months, five 8-hour days a week putting my manuscript on one of my daughter's computers. When this was finished, it was almost time to go back to Florida for the winter. I thought to myself, "You are almost eighty years old. Who knows whether you will be around in the spring to make the refinements you want to make." So I had twenty copies printed, which I sent to relatives, and a few close friends. When I returned to Maryland in 1993, the grim reaper having stayed his hand, I made the corrections I wanted to make and in the reprint I put pictures of the people and the places mentioned in the book. In 1995 I had the book bound in hard copy. To me it is the most beautiful book in the world. I have placed it in the Library of Congress for future generations to read.

And so life marches on. Many, I can almost say most, of my relatives and friends both old and new are gone. May they rest in peace. They, as I have said, enriched my life as I hope I did theirs. A completely new generation has come into being. My beautiful granddaughter, April, has grown up, married, and presented me with two great-grandchildren as beautiful as herself. What a blessing Derek and Amber are in these later years.

As my old friends die, it becomes increasingly difficult to replace them. In a true sense they can never be replaced. But new friends can be made. I know from experience that friends can be made at any age if we are willing to make the effort. On September 12, 1996 I hit the jackpot. I heard that Winona and Fred Ackerman were starting a writers' group at Bowie City Hall. I determined to join the group. There were eight present at my first meeting in addition to myself. They were Winona and Fred Ackerman, Anna Schick, Fran Hutchison, Gerald La Roche, Mary Panneton, Shirley Galusky, and one other whose name I do not have who left the group shortly after it started. What sweet people they were and how talented! I soon found that most were well educated. Several had earned doctorates. Several were poets. All had had interesting experiences which they wrote about and read to the group. I had brought the hardbound copy of my autobiography with me with the hope of making an impression. I was accepted anyhow. Since this first meeting several others have joined the group. Charles Castilla and Alfred Stanglam are among others who have made important contributions to the group. Attendance at the group has become the highlight of my week. As Red Skelton, who recently died, would conclude his programs I say, "May God Bless."

[*Editor's note: The story inspired by the trip to Alaska titled "The Saga of Rainbow Lake" is included in this volume. "Chicken Soup" is included in the volume titled "Franklin Park." The accounts of Ray Theuret's years with the Army Audit Agency are included in the volume titled "Army Audit Days" and also in the longer work, "The Life and Times of Ray Theuret."*]

Sentimental

Written in 1997

My daughter Bonnie laughs at me because I am sentimental. But I know she is glad that I am. I cannot be otherwise, although on occasion, I have tried to be less so. I never succeed and in the end, in a sentimental situation, I feel my chin quivering, my voice choking, and tears welling up in my eyes.

My sentimentality is limited to the living or prior living and does not include objects such as houses or automobiles or clothes or any other of my inanimate possessions.

For example, I have owned and lived in eight different houses during my married life. I have no desire to live in any of the first seven again. I am very happy with my present dwellings, a house in Bowie and an apartment in Florida for the winter.

I feel no sentiment at all when I get rid of my car for a new one although it may have given me faithful service for many years. "Away with the old junker," I say. "Hurrah for the new car," I say.

I feel the same about clothes. I have had favorite garments, which I wore more than others because I thought they make me appear attractive or because they felt comfortable. When they begin to show wear, without a wisp of sentiment, I take them to the Salvation Army or throw them in the trash.

My daughter Bonnie, although a loving person, is not sentimental in the way that I am. She once had two dogs, Benji and Benji's mother Angel. She loved these dogs when they were alive. She carefully attended to them seeing that they were properly fed and taking them to the veterinarian at the slightest sign of illness. She worried about them almost as you would a child. I told her once that I hoped she would feel as bad when I died as she would when they died. I need not have been concerned. When Benji and Angel died, she immediately got two new dogs and Benji and Angel were soon forgotten.

When she was twelve years old, I got Bonnie her first dog. She took good care of her for six years. Then she went off to college and within one year got married. She gave dear Tippy not a thought. When Bonnie visited us on one occasion, after Tippy had grown old and half blind, Tippy did not recognize her. She barked at Bonnie as she would have at the mailman or a passing car. Bonnie was somewhat taken back. I told her that she got her just deserts for neglecting Tippy.

I took care of Tippy for the next eight years. I still feel sad when I think about the time I took her to the veterinarian and had her put to sleep. She had become infirm and half blind. Thirty-five years has passed since that time. I still carry a picture of Tippy in my wallet. I have never had another dog.

Nostalgia is a kin to sentimentalism. The dictionary says: "*nostalgia*—A sentimental memory of or longing for things of the past."

I have little longing for the things of the past. But I am nostalgic about its memories. I remember with pleasure my brother Roy and I, with our friend Walt Fuhrman, tramping the fields and woods around Erie, Pennsylvania especially in the wintertime when we trapped for muskrats. We made a little spending money this way.

Walt moved away when Roy and I were 16 years old and he was 20. He moved with his family to Michigan. We kept in touch with him throughout the years with letters, Christmas cards and occasional visits. I had a long talk with Walt on the telephone on his 86th birthday about three weeks before he died.

My father was a hard workingman. He worked on the railroad on a gang that repaired bridges and tunnels. It was hard physical labor. At his funeral, as I viewed him in his casket, I particularly looked at his large hands. I thought about how hard he had worked with those hands to support me and rest of his family for which I doubt he ever received a single verbal thank you.

I think of my mother and her kindness and love for her family. I remember the time my high school football team beat its heated rival in the last game of the season on Thanksgiving. When I got home from the game I was still very excited but there was nobody to talk to but Mother. She was making pumpkin pies for Thanksgiving and knew nothing about football and couldn't have cared less. But because I was so excited and happy about the game she gave me a whole pumpkin pie to eat by myself.

Ray's photo of Tippy was in his wallet until the end of his life.

We may live only for the present day if we desire. We can give little thought to what has gone on in the past if we wish. But to me memories of the past make the present a happier time. Call it sentimentality or nostalgia, as I have grown old, it makes me look back on my life with a greater feeling of contentment.

Things We Should Say to Each Other

This essay was delivered to the Bowie writer's group on October 20, 1998.

One of the most difficult things for many people to say is, "I love you." I know many people who are just unable to get the words out although they really are loving people. I told my mother and my sisters many times that I loved them, but I never did say this to my father or my brother. I am sure they knew I loved them, but I never told them in so many words. I wish I had.

What magical words they are. The words "I love you" can stop animosity in its tracks. They can end disputes before they start or end them after they begin. They can turn enemies into friends. The words, once spoken, can establish friendships for a lifetime. They can prevent misunderstandings from being acrimonious disputes. They can cement marriages and make divorce unthinkable.

I had a friend once who was being laid out unmercifully by his wife when I was visiting them. In the middle of her tirade he said, "You know I love you." It stopped her in her tracks. As far as I know they haven't had a cross word since, at least in front of me.

The words "I love you" have many synonyms. Let me give a few examples.

Say, "Dad, I appreciate all that you have done for me," as you give him a little hug.

Say, "Mother, you are the best mother in the world," as you give her a peck on the check.

Say, "I'm lucky to have you for a brother and/or a sister."

Say, "I think you are beautiful as you greet your wife in the morning."

Say to your children, "God gave you to me as a precious gift."

Say, "I'm glad I have you for a friend," as you shake his hand.

Say, "It was a fortunate day for me when I met you people," when you come to your weekly writers group.

There are many others too numerous to list.

The point I want to make is that we should take every opportunity to tell the people we love and those we associate with that they are important to us and that we have affection for them. Needless to say, none of this will make our relationships with others as they should be unless, when we say these words, they represent our true sentiments.

Learning To Use the Internet

Written in 2000 when the author was 87 years old.

For several years my daughter has been urging me to learn how to use the Internet.

In reply to her urgings, I said, "Bonnie, I am 87 years old. I am too old to learn something so complicated. You can't teach an old dog new tricks."

"You learned to use the computer to write your stories," she said. "No reason you can't learn to send e-mail and surf the Internet."

"I don't know. I think I need all the cells I have left in my brain to remember the things I already know. I don't think I have enough cells left to absorb much more information. You know, Bonnie, I was born in horse and buggy days when few people had telephones or automobiles and radio was unknown. I have spent my whole life in an age that has had a technological advancement greater than in all the rest of recorded history. For eighty-seven years my brain has been absorbing details about new developments in automobiles, radio, television, airplanes, computers and much more. I don't think it has any space left for the Internet."

"Forget some of the out of date and now useless information you have learned in the past and use the space in your brain for something new like the Internet," she said.

"I forget things easily enough without deliberately trying to," I replied.

My daughter is a persuasive person so I gave her back the old obsolete computer she had given me to write on and ordered a new iMac. When it arrived, she hooked me up to "America On

Line" and announced that I was now on the Internet.

"Great," I said. "Now what do I do?"

"The first thing I'll show you is how to send e-mail; it's simple."

She took the mouse and started moving the curser around.

"First you have to connect your computer with the Internet."

She put the curser on the apple in the left hand corner of the screen and moved it down a couple of spaces to a line that said "America On Line" and clicked it. A new image came on the screen.

She handed me the mouse. "Click where it says **Sign on.**"

I did. The computer started to moan and groan.

"What's that noise?" I said. "Sounds like the computer is going to blow up."

" The computer is just connecting itself to the Internet," she replied. "We must wait until this noise stops before we go on."

The noise eventually stopped, a new image appeared on the screen, and a loud voice said, WELCOME.

"Welcome to what?" I asked. The computer did not answer but Bonnie did.

"Welcome to the Internet. You are now on the Internet ready to send a message to whomever you like. Who do you want to send a message to?"

I reached for my address book.

"Those addresses won't do. You have to have an e-mail address. Everybody on the Internet has a different address. Yours is raytheuret@aol.com. Mine is bonnie4101@aol.com. You can send me a message and when I get home I will answer it."

"See at the top of the screen the word 'Write.' Click on it."

I did. The image on the screen changed.

"In the block which says 'from/to' type in my e-mail address."

"Ok."

"Below is a small block which says 'Subject.' Type in First message."

"Ok."

"In the large block below type in whatever message you want to send to me."

I type, "Thanks, Bonnie, for helping me to learn how to send e-mail."

"If that is all you want to send, you can click on 'send now,' but if you want to send me one of your stories you can click on 'attach' and the titles of your stories will come up on the screen. Click on the story you want to send and then click on 'send now.' In a few seconds the message on the screen will say, 'Your mail has been sent.' and you click on OK. When I get home I can take your message and story off my computer. Simple isn't it?"

"Well, not as difficult as I thought. But how do I receive e-mail?"

"At the top of the screen is a box. Underneath it says Mail Center. Click on it."

I did.

A new image came on the screen.

"Click on mail box."

I did.

Another new image came across the screen.

"Click on new or old messages; you have no messages now, but when you do, the messages you have received will be listed on the screen. Double click on them one at a time and the message will appear at the bottom of the screen. You can print them out on your printer if you wish. If you want to reply click on the box that says 'reply,' type in your reply, and click on 'send now.' That isn't so hard, is it?"

"Not too bad."

A little while after Bonnie went home, following the above instructions, I received my first e-mail. As Bonnie said, it was simple. In this complicated world of ours life gets more simple all the time. Oh yes!

I am now able to send out and receive e-mail and am starting to learn how to take advantage of the many other opportunities available to me on the Internet. Who knows, maybe some day I will be able to send viruses out to my friends, whatever they are.

Mice

This essay was delivered to the Bowie Writers' group on June 20, 2000.

In 1942, after being transferred to York, Pennsylvania by the Army, for whom I worked as a civilian, I rented a second-floor flat, into which I moved my wife, Alice, and four-year-old daughter, Bonnie.

Our landlords, an elderly couple who had years before migrated to America from Sicily, lived on the first floor. The landlords' daughter, Mary, lived on the third floor with her husband, Joe Morello. Incidentally, we became close friends with Mary and Joe and still retain a close relationship with Mary, who now lives near us in Pompano Beach, Florida. Joe is deceased. He was a dear man.

My story today is not related to our relationship with Mary and Joe, but with quite a different subject, mice.

Our flat had a good-sized kitchen with a small porch off the rear. Next to the kitchen was a small sitting room and off the sitting room a bedroom. Off the bedroom in the front of the house was the living room, which we seldom used.

A couple of days after we moved into the flat, Alice told me that a mouse had jumped out of the oven when she opened it and nearly scared her to death. An elephant's fear of mice is only slight apprehension compared to Alice's. "I will buy a mouse trap and catch it," I told Alice. "Don't worry about the mouse; it won't hurt you."

In retrospect, I still feel sorry for that mouse and its many relatives. They had no knowledge when they moved into that house and found what they thought was safe refuge that the second floor flat would eventually be rented to an old muskrat trapper who had lost none of his trapping wiles.

The day after Alice saw the mouse, I bought a mousetrap. That evening, after the dinner dishes had been cleared away, I set the trap in the kitchen, baited it with cheese, and repaired to the sitting room to read the paper.

I had no more than sat down and opened the paper when I heard a snap. I had caught the mouse. I threw it off the back porch into the yard.

I told Alice that she could stop worrying about the mouse she saw, as it was now dead. I also told Alice that I would reset the trap again in the unlikely case the one I had caught had a mate.

I had no more than repaired to the sitting room and my paper again when I heard another snap. After disposing of this catch in the same way I had the first, I reset the trap again in case the pair I had caught had children.

I had a busy evening. I caught eight mice that evening. During that day and the following ones, I caught a total of twenty-eight mice. I caught them all, or else those I didn't catch took fright and moved out. At least we never saw any more mice during the nearly two years we lived in our York second-floor flat.

I was reminded last week of the mice we had in York in 1942 when Alice told me that a mouse had jumped out of the oven at her at our house here in Bowie. She is still as apprehensive of mice as ever. I could hardly believe her. I couldn't see how a mouse could get into our house. I bought two mousetraps at Hardware City. I am glad to report that I have lost none of my trapping wiles. Skills we learn in childhood should be retained. You never know when you will need them. I have caught three mice so far. I have caught none in the last four days. I think I have caught them all. However, I will keep the traps set and baited for a few more days just in case.

My Busy Day

This essay was published in the Bowie Blade-News in 2001.

Years ago, when I was contemplating retirement, I wondered
what I could do to fill up the days then occupied with my
employment. I need not have worried. It was not long after
I retired before my days were so filled with activity that I
wondered how I had ever had time to work.

I moved to Florida for the winter. I took up golf, joined a
bowling team at my condominium, went to the pool nearly every
day, played bingo, attended condominium parties, visited and
went out to dinner with relatives and friends and entertained
a lot of visitors from up north. When I returned north for the
summer and fall, I continued my golf, visited back and forth with
relatives and friends, joined in senior citizen center activities, and
took trips, both domestically and overseas. I became so busy that
I began to look forward to a period of time or even a day or two
when I would have nothing to do.

As the years went by and I arrived at age eighty, I found
that I had to reduce my activities. A few years ago, I told a close
friend that I had made my mind up to do only one thing a day.
For example, on my Senior Writers' Group day, I would plan to
do nothing else. If I played golf, I would do nothing else that day.
I have succeeded in reducing my activities but recently I have had
a complete relapse.

I took my wife and a friend to Paint Branch Golf Complex.
Paint Branch has only nine holes and we walked. We left the
house at 7 a.m. and were back home by 10 a.m. Incidentally,
I played well except for one hole I messed up. I had five pars,
which was the best I have done in several years. According to my

reduced activity plan, this should have been "it" for the day except for reading or watching television. But this was not to be.

The day before I had received a Maryland Vehicle Emissions Inspection Notice on our 1987 Nova. I wasn't tired from my golf, and as it was still early in the day when I got home, I thought, "I might as well get the inspection out of the way so I have one less thing to worry about." The notice said, "See enclosed brochure for exact locations of VEIP testing stations." I checked the brochure, and the address where I had previously taken the Nova for inspection was listed. When I got there, I couldn't find it. I learned, by making inquiry at a Mercury Dealer nearby, that it had moved. I assume the State of Maryland, trying to economize because of concern for its citizens' taxes, was just using up the brochures on hand after the station moved. The new emissions station was only about two miles away from the old one. After a few wrong turns, I found it. The Nova passed inspection, and on taking my $12 the attendant wished me a nice day.

My day was far from over. I knew I had to drive my wife to John Hopkins in Baltimore the next day for her annual eye examination. I knew I was low on gas in my Mercury, which I would be driving to Baltimore. So after I drove the Nova into the garage, I got into the Mercury and went to the gas station. My lawnmower gas can was empty, so I thought I might as well get some gas for the lawnmower while I was at it. The gas station was just across the street from my bank, so I decided to go to the bank and get our monthly cash, which we use for groceries and miscellaneous other cash purchases.

I had broken the mirror on the right hand side of the Mercury a couple of days before. While I was out, I thought I might as well drive over to Route 3 to a glass place that I had done business with before and see if I could get a new mirror.

I drove up and down Route 3, but I couldn't find it. They had either moved or gone out of business. I was low on computer paper, and as long as I was on Route 301 or 3 -- I don't know where one ends and the other begins -- I thought I might as well go to Staples and get some computer paper. Staples had a sale, buy three and get one free, so I bought four reams of paper for the price of three.

When I got home, it was 3:30 p.m. I had been on the run since 7 a.m., and I must say, much of it under stressful conditions. As I drove into the garage, I thought, "Maybe I can take it easy for the rest of the day." I was wrong.

My wife had bought one of those TV stands that you have to put together. There is nothing I hate to do more than put one of these stands together. I generally put them together wrong and have to take them apart and put them together again and there always seem to be missing parts or parts left over. However, this stand was relatively uncomplicated and I only made one mistake in putting it together. All the parts were there except for one nail. The brochure said 11 nails, but there were only 10 in the package. One less nail didn't make any difference. The only mistake I made in assembly was that I put the top on wrong way. It didn't look so bad that way, but I knew if my son-in-law came over and saw it, he would laugh at me for putting the stand together wrong, so I took the top off and put it on right.

So at last my activities for the day ended. I knew I would be busy the next day because I had to drive my wife to John Hopkins in Baltimore, but that is another day.

The Baseball Fan

This essay was delivered to the Bowie writers' group on May 1, 2001.

Since I was a small boy, I have been interested in major
league baseball. I have watched thousands of games on television
or listened to descriptions of them on radio. I have gone to
ballgames whenever I could. I still do.

When I was working, I traveled extensively. Many of the
cities I visited had major league baseball teams. In the evenings,
rather than sitting around in hotels, I attended baseball games
when possible. I spent many pleasant evenings at ballparks,
saw many interesting games and many great players perform.
One game I attended I will never forget, although the reason I
remember it has little to do with the game itself.

I was in Pittsburgh for a few days on this occasion. My hotel
was not far from Forbes Field, which was, at the time, the home
ballpark of the Pittsburgh Pirates. It was a pleasant evening and
since, as usual, I had nothing to do in the evening, I walked over
to the ballpark and bought a ticket. Immediately in front of me
in the ticket line was a little man with a bag of beer. He was
obviously already three sheets to the wind. I thought, "I hope he
doesn't sit next to me."

After buying my ticket, I walked leisurely to my seat. It was
second from the aisle. I was glad I didn't have the aisle seat for it
was directly behind a huge steel pillar that hid a good part of the
field from view. The modern baseball stadiums now being built
have eliminated such obstructions.

A few minutes before the game was to start, I saw in the
distance the little man with the bag of beer walking in my
general direction. I thought to myself again, "I hope he doesn't

sit next to and spill beer on me." But with thousands of empty seats, I thought the chance was remote. But, relentlessly he approached, and when he came to my aisle, he started up the steps and when he reached my row of seats, he sat down next to me in the seat behind the steel pillar. If I had been him I would have immediately returned to the ticket window and demanded a better seat. But he sat down without complaint. He was humming a little tune.

Settled in his seat, still humming his little tune, he bent down to his bag of beer, which he had placed between his feet, and took out a bottle. He looked up at me and offered me a bottle of beer. I thanked him, but said no.

When the national anthem was sung, he arose and put his hand over his heart. The song over, he peeked around the pillar in front of him, and in a weak voice, joined the rest of the crowd in hollering, "play ball." As the game proceeded, he sat behind the pillar sipping his beer. Every once in a while, he would peek around the pillar and give a little cheer for the home team.

By the fourth inning, the beer caught up with him. He picked up his bag containing his remaining full bottles, as well as the empties, and headed for the place of relief. I watched him as he walked down the steps. I was happy when he made it to the bottom without falling. He slowly walked to an entrance that went under the stadium. I expected that this would be the last I would see of him.

The game proceeded while my beer-drinking friend was absent from his seat. Ralph Kiner, future member of the Baseball Hall of Fame at Cooperstown, hit a home run. Alas, he didn't get to see it. Along about the seventh inning, contrary to my expectations, I saw him emerge from under the stands and slowly walk towards the section where his seat was located. He climbed the stairs without falling and sat down in his seat behind the pillar. His bag now contained only two beers. He had disposed of the empties. Before taking one of the remaining bottles of beer from his bag he peeked around the pillar and gave a cheer of encouragement to the home team.

He rationed his beer so that as the last out was made he finished his last beer. The game over, he put the empty bottle in his bag, rose unsteadily to his feet and headed slowly to the exit. He again maneuvered the steps without falling. He turned in one direction, I in another.

He was a nice little man. Despite my apprehension when he sat down in the seat next to me, I can report that he didn't spill a single drop of beer on me. It is fans like him that has made baseball the great sport to watch that it is.

The First Day of The Rest of My Life

*This essay was delivered to the writers' group at Lighthouse Point,
Florida when the author was 89 years old.*

Each morning as we arouse ourselves from slumber, we are
starting the first day of the rest of our lives. Each day we must
make many decisions, few more important than those we make
the first half-hour of our day.

My day begins with the realization that I am awake. I have
been dreaming. I can't remember what my dream was about. I
wish I could. It was a pleasant dream. If I go back to sleep, maybe
it will return.

But I see the room is full of light. Day has arrived. I probe
the other side of the bed with my foot. I feel nothing. Alice
is already up. Where does that 84-year-old woman get such
energy? I wonder if she has gone to the pool where a few of the
condominium early birds gather each morning. No. I hear her
moving around in the kitchen. I bet she is making cookies again.
I think I smell them. I sometimes think she should stop making
so many cookies. Lead me not into temptation. My doctor says
I shouldn't eat cookies because of my diabetes. What does he
know? Alice's cookies are so good. You can't buy cookies like
them in the stores. I'll only eat two this morning. That won't hurt
me. I wonder which of Alice's friends in the condominium are
going to benefit from this bake.

If I thought I could go back to sleep, I would turn over on
my other side and sleep for another half-hour. But I know I can't
get back to sleep. I am too wide-awake. I turn over on my back.

I make my 1st decision of the day. Should I do those exercises
that the bone doctor said would lessen the ache in my hips? I hate

the exercises. I decide to do them anyway. I put my hand below my knees and pull them forward as far as I can at the same time bending my back forward as far as I can. The doctor said to do this 10 times. I count one, two, three — I lose track of the count. I think one or two more or less won't make any difference.

After my exercises, I lay back on the bed, resting. I think again about trying to go back to sleep, but decide it would be useless to try. Tentatively, I put one leg over the side of the bed, and then the other. I sit up slowly and rub my eyes. I wonder if I will be woozy when I stand up like I was day before yesterday. I grab hold of the bureau in front of me and slowly rise to my feet. I let go of the bureau. No, I'm not woozy this morning. "Thanks, God," I say looking up.

It is time for the 2nd decision of the day. Should I make the bed? Should I ask Alice to come in and help? It is a king-sized bed. It is a lot easier to make if there are two people making it, one on each side of the bed. But Alice is making cookies. I guess I had better make it myself. I pull the sheet and the blanket up on my side. I then creep over to Alice's side of the bed and do the same. I also pull the bedspread up on Alice's side. Then back to my side. I notice that I have not pulled the bedspread up far enough on Alice's side of the bed. I go over to her side again and make an adjustment. I pulled too much, so I have to go back to my side and make an other adjustment. I still haven't got the sides exactly even, but I decide it is good enough. I put the four colorful cushions on the bed that Alice wants on it after it is made. I sit on the edge of the bed and rest before my next move.

I open a bureau drawer to take out a clean pair of undershorts. Decision No. 3. What color of under shorts do I want to wear today? I make a decision, blue. Decision No. 4. What slacks or shorts am I going to wear today? I decide tan slacks and open another bureau drawer and take out a pair of clean socks to match.

I start for my bathroom at the other side of the living room. I walk slowly holding on to the door frame, and then the organ, and then the dining room chairs with the hand not encumbered with the undershorts and socks. My den is next to my bathroom and my closet is next to my den. I throw the clean socks into the den and go into my bathroom.

After answering nature's call, I take out my toothbrush and a tube of toothpaste. I notice that there isn't much toothpaste in the tube and vaguely think, "I must go to the drugstore and get some more. No, I am fully awake now; I will ask Alice to get it when she goes to the food store. That way it will come out of the grocery money and not from my allowance."

I squeeze the top of the tube and enough paste comes out for the needs of this day. I brush my teeth and the ooze comes out over my chin. I wipe it off with a Kleenex and scrub my teeth a little more. I rinse my mouth and bend down for the mouthwash in the lower cabinet. I feel my hips aching a little.

I move to the shower door. I reach in and turn on the shower and wait a second for the cold water in the pipes to be replaced by the hot water before I climb in. I turn my back to the shower. The hot water beats against my lower back and hips. It feels good. I can feel the ache going away. I put shampoo on my head and rub it into my hair and then rinse. I realize that I need a haircut. I rub soap over my body and sit down on the bath stool and wash my feet. I sit there awhile as the water washes the soapsuds and the aches away. I grab hold of the hand bar and rise to my feet and turn the water off.

I step out of the shower. I forgot to get a bath towel out of the linen closet. I now have my first communication of the day with Alice. Alice is still in the kitchen. I yell, "Alice, I forgot a towel." I hide behind the bathroom door in modesty as Alice hands me a towel through the eight-inch crack of the door I have opened. I towel myself dry and sit on the toilet seat and put on my clean blue under shorts. I open the door and wipe off the mist that has settled on the mirror so I can see to comb my hair, which is tangled from the shower. Yes, I will have to get a haircut one of these days.

My hair combed, I waddle into the kitchen. This is Alice's first sight of me that day except for my arm when I reached for the towel. She survives. She is neatly groomed as always. The cookies baking in the oven smell good.

One chore remains before I can be declared alive. I have to take my pills and take my blood sugar. I get the pill case out. I have put a week's allotment of the pills I have to take into the slots of the case, three slots for each day. I dump the morning allotments into my hand and gulp them down with a glass of water. I get my diabetic testing equipment out and prick my finger. A little spot of blood appears. The reading this morning is 102. Perfect. That doctor is a fanatic about cookies. I knew those cookies I ate before I went to bed would do me no harm.

Alice said, "What do you want for breakfast? Stop eating those cookies. They will ruin your breakfast."

I reply, "I'll only eat two. Let's go out for breakfast?"

"Where?"

I make my 5th decision of the morning. "The Pancake House."

"OK, when do you want to go?"

"As soon as I get dressed, read the paper and check yesterday's stock market to see if we can afford it."

So begins a typical first day of the rest of my life.

Mirror, Mirror On The Wall

This essay was first delivered to the writers' group at Lighthouse Point, Florida on February 13, 2001 when the author was 89 years old.

Mirror, mirror on the wall, who is the most handsome man of all? Early in life, I knew it wasn't going to be me. Although I didn't consider myself ugly or even homely, there were a few changes I would have made in my physical makeup if I had had my druthers.

When I was a boy, I was small and skinny. At age fifteen I was five feet two inches tall and weighed 100 pounds. I didn't start growing until I was nearly sixteen. At one time my twin brother Roy was four inches taller than me and 25 pounds heavier. When I graduated from high school at age 18, I was five feet seven inches tall and weighed 115 pounds. In the three years after I graduated, I gained three more inches in height but only about 10 additional pounds in weight. I was 24 years old before I finally began to gain some weight, which made me very happy at the time. At my largest I was five feet ten inches tall and weighed 180 pounds. I have shrunk some since.

When I was in junior high, we were required to take swimming. We swam in the nude. The teacher made us stand in line at the edge of the pool. I hated this. I was well aware of how my skinny little frame compared to those who were beginning to develop into large, strong, muscular boys. When I went into the 9th grade (in high school), swimming was not a requirement, so I no longer had to face the embarrassment of standing naked with the other boys by the pool.

I would have loved to be as big as I am now when I went to school. I could then have gone out for football. For my size I was a pretty good athlete, but at a little over 100 pounds until I was in the 12th grade, football was out of the question. I could have played baseball, but my school didn't have a baseball team.

In addition to maturing late, there were some other things I would have changed if I could have had a choice. I will mention only a few.

I would have liked to be six feet tall. Actually, I would have liked to be at least six feet one half-inch tall. Then I could have said, if asked, "I am over six feet tall."

Until my hair turned white, I have always disliked my hair. My father had black hair, which laid flat on his head. I wished when I was growing up that my hair had taken after his family rather than that of my mother, who had thick auburn hair. My hair was reddish brown and always stood up on end. Smoothing it down with water did little good. As soon as the water evaporated, my hair would jump back up. When I was young, I never considered hairdressing. We had no money to spend on anything so frivolous. I doubt it would have helped anyway.

My father cut my hair until I was in high school. He had only hand sheers and they would grab and pull at my hair and I would squirm and complain. Sometimes my father would get disgusted and stop cutting and I would be left with half a haircut. It really didn't make much difference. There wasn't much you could do with my hair anyway. About the time I entered high school, a man who cut hair in his spare time moved into our neighborhood and he cut my hair for 15 cents. The improvement was only minor.

My teeth were a concern to me when I was young. I have good strong teeth, although not straight. I lost three teeth to decay in my teens because my family could not afford dental care. I lost only one more after I got a job and went to a dentist on a regular basis. In this day and age, I would have lost no teeth when I was young and with today's orthodontics would have had straight and attractive teeth. This would have made a difference to me when I was young.

I wonder if anybody beside myself, when they get up in

Daddy's favorite photo of himself.

years, ever looks back and wonders at what period in life they were their most attractive. I would guess that with most, it would be in their late teens or early 20s. However, there are "ugly ducklings when they were young" that as they mature and age, grow into beautiful people. Eleanor Roosevelt once said, "Beautiful young people are accidents of nature, but beautiful old people are works of art."

When I published my autobiography, I decided that at age 47, I had reached my attractive peak and I put a photo of myself from that period on the cover of my book.

One further thought and I will close. Among the many things that I like about the writers groups that I attend is that you can write and read anything, no matter how personal, or how ridiculous, and you will receive sympathy and understanding from the other members of the group.

Nine One-One

This essay was delivered to the Bowie Senior Writers' Group on September 18, 2001.

In my lifetime, the United States has been involved in four great wars. In all these wars, with the exception of Pearl Harbor, the physical devastation suffered by other countries did not touch our own shores. The terrorists' attacks last Tuesday were the first time that American civilians, while living in their own country, have been targeted for attack. In the instance of Pearl Harbor, the attack was primarily on the military, not on civilians.

Like most of you, I have been glued to the television since I returned home from our meeting last week. I have been wondering how these attacks are going to affect my country and the people I love. I know that it is unlikely to affect me personally, for I am an old man who will soon, as the saying goes, be leaving this vale of tears. But I wonder how it will affect Derek and Amber, my great-grandchildren, and my nephews and nieces and their offspring, and those of friends who I hold dear. I wonder if they will continue to enjoy the benefits of liberty and freedom, which have been a part of my life.

First I want to put the terrorist Tuesday attacks in perspective. Truly, they were horrendous. But they were minor in comparison with others that have taken place in my lifetime. I remember when London was bombed nightly for months on end. I remember when we firebombed Tokyo and incinerated 83,000 civilian men, women and children in a single raid. I remember when the British firebombed Hamburg and at least 50,000 perished. I need not mention Hiroshima and Nagasaki. All these atrocities were performed by governments of so-called

Christian nations, not by crazed Muslim fanatics. I do not believe we should overly magnify evil simply because it falls on us.

What I have been hearing on television is not heartening. Jingoism is in full cry. I heard many shouts of rage on TV and the hope expressed over and over again that we start bombing immediately. I heard one man say, "I hope we start immediately to bomb the hell out of them."

When asked who 'they' were, he had no answer. On a talk show, I watched a man ask this simple question. "How do we know that Osama bin Laden was responsible for the bombings?" The lady host cut him off short and the audience clapped when she did so. It is now apparently un-American to have the slightest doubt that bin Laden was involved. Personally, I think he was. He is certainly qualified. I believe he worked with the CIA during the Cold War and took over the terrorist network that we had developed when the Soviet Union fell apart.

True, I heard some words of moderation, but not from most of our political leaders, including the President. In fact, I have heard just the opposite. I have the feeling that they are all very happy to have been relieved from the problems of maintaining a surplus, paying off the national debt and saving social security. The war cry now, in addition to bombing the hell out of somebody, will be spend-spend-spend.

The actions of our leader, the President, will largely determine how our country survives the present crisis. Plato said that right action -- he called it justice -- is a combination of virtue and wisdom. To this, I would add a need to be strong. At such times as we now face, our country needs a leader who has all these attributes. I do not question the desire of our President to do what is best for our country. But, does he have the wisdom to make the right choices? And, above all, is he strong enough to resist the Jingoistic advice he will be receiving from our military and from the politicians who are only interested in winning the next election?

I tremble as I look to the future.

Nostalgia

This essay was first delivered to the Bowie Senior Writers' Group on September 26, 2000.

Vice President Gore was recently asked the following question during one of his news conferences: "What is the most nostalgic memory you have of the period when you were growing up." After a little thought he replied, "It was playing ball with my father." I don't know whether Governor Bush was ever asked this question. But if he was, he could well have given the same answer. His father, President Bush, was a good ball player. He played first base for Yale when he attended there.

When I heard the above question to Vice President Gore, I thought, "What answer would I give if that question was asked of me?" My answer would have been, "Trapping muskrats with my twin brother Roy after we moved to Franklin Park in February 1925, when we were 12 years old."

Franklin Park is a small settlement of brick row houses built during the Great War to house defense workers. It is at the very city limits of Erie, Pennsylvania. In between this settlement and the built up part of Erie, at that time, were several creeks and cattail swamps that are the natural habitat of muskrats. Roy and I had a name for each of these swamps: Carbarn Swamp, 10th Street Swamp, 12th Street Swamp, and the most important, the G. E. Swamp.

The General Electric bought a piece of land approximately one mile by one half-mile wide just outside the Erie city limits when they built their Erie plant in the early 20th century. They built the plant outside the city limits of Erie in order to avoid paying city taxes. In between the Erie city limits and the first

G.E. plant building were open fields and cattail swamps. During the 2nd World War, the G.E. expanded its Erie plant, and since that time, part of our most important muskrat trapping grounds have been covered with large red brick buildings.

The Twins: Roy and Ray Theuret as young men, the bond begun in childhood is still of great importance.

Just across the street from us when we moved to Franklin Park lived a boy named Bill Duel, who had just turned 16 years old. On becoming 16, he had quit school and obtained a job in a local plant. He had been trapping muskrats in the swamps around Franklin Park, and he told Roy he could take over his trap lines if he wanted to. Roy bought Bill's traps, and Bill instructed him on how to go about trapping. The legal trapping season ended on February 28th, and Roy did not succeed in catching any muskrats before the season ended.

When the legal trapping season started that fall, on November 1st, Roy was ready. He had scouted the swamps and streams around Franklin Park and knew which of them had muskrats. That summer, I bought a paper route. So, the winter of 1925-1926, while Roy trapped, I delivered papers. Muskrat skins, at the time, sold to fur dealers for an average of about $1.50 per skin. I do not remember how many muskrats Roy caught that winter, but I believe he made as much money, maybe more, trapping as I did delivering papers.

I kept my paper route until the fall of 1926, at which time I decided to get rid of the route and join Roy on the trap line. Trapping muskrats seemed much more interesting to me than delivering papers every day to people who sometimes wouldn't even pay me. I used the money I had earned delivering papers to buy some muskrat traps and a pair of rubber boots that I would need in order to wade around in the swamps. I also bought a kerosene lantern since it would still be dark when I looked at my traps each morning.

That fall, Roy and I spent Saturdays and Sundays wading around in swamps and creeks, prospecting for signs of muskrats that we could follow up on when the season opened on November 1st. We waited impatiently for the season to open. The 31st of October, Halloween, finally arrived. We set our traps just before dark that evening. Legally we were not supposed to set our traps until 12:01 a. m. on November 1st, but we jumped the gun a few hours. That first evening, we set our traps only in the Carbarn Swamp and in the G.E. Swamp.

That evening, Roy and I were so excited, we could hardly sleep. We planned on getting up by 5:30 a.m., but we woke up early. We put on our boots, and with our lanterns, were on the way to look at our traps by 5 a.m. I caught two muskrats in the Carbarn Swamp and Roy caught one. Roy caught two muskrats in the G.E. Swamp, but I caught none there. We were back home by 6 a.m. after what we thought was a very successful start to the trapping season. Between us that first day, Roy and I made over $7, which was a lot of money to us at the time. Trapping muskrats provided us spending money and money for clothes, which we would not otherwise have had.

All that winter and for the following two years, Roy and I trapped muskrats around Franklin Park during school days. On weekends and during the holiday periods -- Thanksgiving and Christmas -- we would go to Six Mile Creek, a stream which was six miles from the center of Erie, thus its name. It was three miles from our home. On weekends, we were joined by our buddy, Walt Fuhrman, who lived in the center of Erie and who was also a trapper. Walt moved to Michigan with his family in 1929. I kept in touch with him over the years. I last talked with him on July 12, 1995, his 86th birthday, about six weeks before he died.

My brother Roy died on December 9, 1988, our 76th birthday. There is never a day that I don't think of him. I was very fortunate to have had him for a brother.

Reincarnation

This essay was delivered first to the Bowie Senior Writers' group on June 19, 2001.

Some religions, principally Asiatic religions such as Hinduism and its offshoot Buddhism, are big on reincarnation. The theory seems to be that there is a mass of energy/spirit in the universe that cannot be distorted. Accordingly, when a man dies, the spirit/energy that he possesses goes into some other life or form of life. This, it is believed, has been going on for millions of years, and each of us has existed in some form many times over the millenniums. According to this belief, when a man dies, his spirit/energy does not necessarily go into another human, but can go into some other form of life, such as an ant or a cow.

A fundamentalist Hindu, someone who would be considered a member of the religious right in this country, will not harm or kill any form of life. He walks very carefully, making sure he does not inadvertently step on and harm any other creature, such as an ant. For alas, if he stepped on and killed an ant, he might be squashing dear old Uncle Mahatma who recently died, and now has come back to this world as an ant. He would not eat meat of any kind. The delicious T-bone steak he might enjoy could have come from a cow that is the reincarnation life of his grandmother who passed away several years ago. Such possibilities probably should give us unbelievers some reason for thought. For the ancients who established the belief in reincarnation might possibly be right.

Judo-Christians and Muslims have another depository for the spirit/energy they have before they die. Rather than using this no longer needed resource to sustain some later form of life, they deposit it in either heaven or hell. Judging by the energy evidenced by the reputed heat in one of these places, I will let you judge where people who are adherents of these beliefs believe most end up.

I am not sure who people that believe in reincarnation think makes the decision as to what kind of creature they will be in their next life. Whom do they believe determines whether they come back as a rich beautiful talented human or an ant? Perhaps they believe you just take potluck. That whatever in nature needs the energy you release when you can no longer use it, gets it. Perhaps many of us unknowingly also harbor such views, and this is the reason so few of us properly use the spirit/energy we have in our current life. Some think you can influence your next life by properly living your current life. But this view, unfortunately, is not generally held.

Assuming that I have some choice as to what kind of life I will have in the next reincarnation, I would choose pretty much what I had in my current existence, with minor changes. I would not want to change my parents or my siblings. I would not change my wife or my children. I would not change the many friends I have had and still have. The minor changes I would like would be generally limited to the following:

1. I would like to have had my parents be a little richer so that my father wouldn't have had to work so hard and would have been able to send me to college.

2. I would have liked to have been bigger when I was in my teens so I could have played high school football.

3. I would like to have had a good ear for music
   and been able to sing like some other bird
   than a crow.

A final thought: Reincarnation as a crow wouldn't be all that bad.
The crow is a mighty smart bird.

Spelling

This essay was delivered to the Bowie Senior Writers' Group in the spring of 2000 when the author was 87 years old.

In order to have something to read to my writers' group, I decided to write about the dinner party I threw for my last birthday. After the guests had assembled in our apartment and before we went to the restaurant for dinner, my wife Alice served the guests several delicious Hor d'oeu-vres. Being the world's worst speller, I immediately ran into trouble by my inability to spell *Hor d'oeu-vres*. I first thought I will change the word to snacks. I can spell snacks. But, I knew "snacks" was not the right word. Snacks are something you have when a dinner will not follow or when you want a little something to chew on while you are watching television. I could say appetizers, but I can't spell that either. As long as I have to look up the spelling in the dictionary, I might as well look up *Hor d'oeu-vres*.

I keep the dictionary close beside me when I am writing, for I know I will have to refer to it frequently. *Hor d'oeu -vres*. O-R-D-U-V-S. That sounds about right. I'll look under the O R s. I put my finger on the page in my dictionary at OR and go down the words starting with or. ORDURE (Getting close), finally the last word under the ORs, O R T O T A N a small European bird. No *Hor d'oeu-vres*. Maybe it's spelled O E R D U V S. The French have a funny way of spelling. I'll look under the O E Rs. The only O E R in the dictionary is O'er, poetical for over.

Well, I guess the only way to find *Hor d'oeu-vres* is to look at all the words in the dictionary starting with O. There are 27 pages of O's in my dictionary. The first word in the O's is Oaf, an awkward lout. The last word is Ozonosphere (the atmosphere region about 25 miles above the earth.) I skip all the words starting with O R and O E R. I do not find *Hor d'oeu-vres*.

I think to myself. This is strange. The word is commonly used. It should be in the dictionary. The cover of the dictionary I am using says "The Oxford American Dictionary." An Englishman named James Murray in the middle of the 19th century first assembled *The Oxford Dictionary*. Maybe Murray didn't like the French and refused to put any words derived from French words in his dictionary. I wish I had a Webster Dictionary, but I don't.

I've spent so much time trying to find how *Hor d'oeu-vres* is spelled that I hate to give up. But, where do I go from here? I guess I'll call my daughter. Bonnie is a good speller and she already knows I am a dumb head as far as spelling is concerned. Ring - Ring - Ring. Come on, somebody answer. I don't have all day. Ring - Ring - Click – Hello, Bonnie? Yes, Daddy, how are you? I'm Ok.

Bonnie, I'm writing a story that I want to read to my writers' group about the birthday party and dinner I threw for myself last December. Bonnie, you know those little hot dogs wrapped in sourdough and baked your mother serves at my parties? I want to call them *Hor d'oeu-vres* in my story, but I can't spell it and it's not in the dictionary. I'm sure it is in the dictionary. No, it isn't. I looked at every word on the 27 pages of O's in the dictionary, and it's not there. Daddy, *Hor d'oeu-vres* doesn't start with an O; it starts with a H. H O R. You sure, Bonnie? It's pronounced Or-Durvs not Hor-Durvs. I'm sure. Daddy. Look under the H's. Ok, H m, H m, Ho. You are right, Bonnie. Boy! what a crazy language. No wonder my great-grandfather left France and came to America where words are spelled like they sound. Thanks, Bonnie. See ya.

At my 87th birthday party, my wife served delicious *Hor d'oeu-vres* to our guests before we all went out to dinner. Next year at my birthday party, I'm not taking them out to dinner, and I'll have Alice serve snacks instead. I can spell snacks. Sorry, folks. Bring presents anyway.

Spud Kelly

One day, when I was eleven years old and in the 5th grade, on coming out of the school I attended in Erie, Pennsylvania, I saw a couple of kids about my age annoying a rather large, clumsy looking kid. They were not too serious about this and when I came up to them, they went away. I started talking to him. His name was Elmer Sheridan Kelly. Elmer was somewhat retarded, and in addition to being naturally clumsy, had limited use of his left shoulder and arm, which had been scalded when he was a baby. I lived only half a block from the school, and I took Elmer home with me.

Mother made a practice of inviting any kid I brought home to the Sunday School we attended, and so she invited Elmer. Elmer said he would come if I would come after him. I was a little reticent about this, but Mother made me go after him the next Sunday. For all the next winter, I had to go after him, otherwise he would not come. He lived in a different direction from the Sunday School than my family did, and this meant that I had to walk an extra two miles each Sunday to and from Sunday school.

The next year, we moved to a different part of town so that I couldn't go for him anymore. However, by this time, his mother had started to attend the church, and Elmer came on his own. He became a regular attendee and seldom missed a Sunday. In fact, he once went seven years without missing a single Sunday.

Mrs. Kelly was a kindly women, and I occasionally went home from Sunday school with Elmer. Mrs. Kelly generally served chicken for dinner and for desert had Jell-O with whipped cream, which I liked. Elmer had a dog, a Boston bull, named Jiggs. There was sometimes dog dirt on the Kellys' floors, which I disliked.

When I went home with Elmer, we played baseball or

football in the afternoon, depending upon the season. Elmer liked all sports and although clumsy and slow, managed to play in a reasonably satisfactory manner. When, later on, the church had a baseball team, Elmer was the catcher because he was big and was not afraid to catch.

Elmer's father was a short man who worked as a watchman at a local plant. Mr. Kelly only came to church once that I remember. However, he came on the day that the congregation had its picture taken, and anybody looking at the picture of the congregation taken at that time would think Mr. Kelly was a pillar of the church. Mr. Kelly was so short that when he drove his car, you could hardly see his head over the dashboard. He also drove fast. How he kept from having a serious accident, I do not know.

I have always been glad that I took the time to get Elmer to go to Sunday school, for it was there he found friends. He would otherwise have had a lonely life. Elmer was treated affectionately by the church people. While he was teased by the kids, it was done in good humor and Elmer enjoyed it. Few people called Elmer by his Christian name. He was known throughout Erie as "Spud" Kelly and was so addressed by his friends.

While crossing a street, Elmer was killed instantly by a car in December 1940. This happened shortly after I moved to Philadelphia. It probably was a mercy. Elmer was then over 30 years old. His friends had all married, and had little time to spend with him. He was increasingly lonely. His mother was growing old, and when she died, there would have been nobody to look out for him.

I sometimes think that on that great day when the goats are separated from the sheep, that if I am kept with the sheep, it will be because I was kind to Elmer "Spud" Kelly.

The Trip

This essay was delivered to the writers' group at Lighthouse Point on March 19, 2001.

In 1922, we lived in the small village of Chapmansville in northwestern Pennsylvania. That summer, my father was assigned by the railroad to a project in Erie. Erie is about 45 miles from Chapmansville. He drove in his 1921 Model T Ford early each Monday morning to Erie and returned home by the same means on Saturday evening.

He knew he wouldn't be able to do this during the winter months, so he and Mother decided to move their family, consisting of four small children, into some furnished rooms in Erie during this period. They planned to return to Chapmansville in the spring.

My twin brother Roy and I, then 9 years old, and sister Edith, 8 years old, could hardly wait for the day of our move. Even Ola, 11 months old, seemed to join in the anticipated excitement of moving to and living in what was, to us, a big city.

We moved on the 3rd Sunday in October on a typical northwestern Pennsylvania warm October day. In the morning, Pa took our old black cat to a farmer who lived about three miles away. He figured it couldn't find its way back to our empty house from that far away. When he returned, we started loading the car with, in addition to our clothing, the bedcovers, dishes, pots and pans and other things we would need in the furnished rooms Pa had rented. By 2 p.m., we were ready to leave. A Model T Ford is not very roomy. To say we were somewhat crowded is an understatement. Roy, Edith and I had to stand up in the back. Ma held Ola on her lap.

Before we started, Ma took one final look around the inside of the house to see if she had overlooked anything she would need in Erie. She had no need to check locks on doors and windows since we had none in our house. They were not needed in our countryside at the time. Pa cranked the car, and we were on our way.

We started north up the dirt road that went by our house. All the roads we would be traveling except the final three or four miles into Erie were dirt. The Model T was pulling hard with the heavy load it was carrying. On some of the little hills out of Chapmansville, Pennsylvania, Pa had to put the car in low gear to carry the hill. When it was in low gear, the car barely crawled.

Although Pa had intended our first stop to be in Union City, half way to Erie, we had to make several stops before we got that far. About halfway to Union City, Edith complained that her leg hurt her. Because of our cramped situation, her leg had gone to sleep.

Ma said, "Stop the car, Clyde, and let Edith stretch her leg."

Pa didn't say anything, but he stopped the car. He looked a little grumpy. "All of you pile out and stretch your legs too," he said. "I don't want to stop again until we reach Union City."

Five minutes later, we were again on the move. We hadn't gone more than three miles before Roy said, "Pa, I have to go bad."

"Me too," I said. In this day and age, we would have used the expression, "I have to go to the bathroom," but up to this time, we had never lived in a house that had a bathroom and the expression was unknown to us.

Pa did not immediately stop the car. "Why didn't you go into the woods and go when Edith was stretching her leg?" Pa said.

"I didn't have to then," Roy replied.

Pa kept on driving. "Stop the car," Ma said. "I don't want them to wet their pants and stink up our clothing and the blankets and sheets packed in with them. Stop the car." Pa muttered something under his breath and stopped the car.

After Pa cranked the car which had stalled, we were on our way again. We were only about three miles from Union City when Ma told Pa to stop the car again. "Ola wet her diaper," she said.

"Annie, can't you wait until we get to Union City to change her?"

"No, I can't hold her away from me so I won't get my dress wet that long and it is too cramped to change it in the car."

Pa muttered something again under his breath and slammed on the brakes. "We will never get to Erie before dark if we stop every five minutes. We are not even half way there and we already have been on the road two hours."

Being Sunday, most of the stores in Union City were closed but the ice-cream parlor was open. Pa bought us all, including himself, an ice cream cone. Ola licked Ma's cone and cooed in happiness. Ma fed her a bottle of milk. Ma told Pa that he should get some gas. Pa wasn't in the mood to take advice from anybody. He shook his head no and said, "Don't need any. I have plenty of gas to get to Erie."

Pa left Union City by the way of Arbuckle, the road he usually traveled from Union City to Erie. But on the road out of Arbuckle, the car couldn't make it to the top of the hill. The Model T had its gas tank under the front seat with a gravity feed gas flow to the engine. As a result of the slant of the hill and the low amount of gas in the tank, not enough gas was getting to the engine to give it the power needed to climb the hill, even in low. The car stalled. Pa got out and cranked it again. The engine started, but it wouldn't move. "I'll have to back the car down the hill and go to Erie another way," he said.

"It's dangerous backing a car down a hill. What if the brakes fail?" Ma said. She ordered us children out of the car.

"I'll be in the car. How about me? Aren't you worried about me?" Pa said and grinned a little.

"I told you to get some gas in Union City," she replied a little tartly. Pa didn't say anything more but he didn't look pleased.

We trudged our way down the hill back into Arbuckle. There we all climbed back into the car and Pa started up another hilly road. This hill also was too much for the car. We almost made it but not quite. Again we all, except Pa, climbed out of the car and trudged our way back down into Arbuckle. Pa backed the car down again.

There are three roads out of Arbuckle, which can be used to reach Erie. This time, after he had turned the car around, Pa backed the car half way up the hill he had just backed down. He then made us all get back into the car, and we went roaring down the hill and through Arbuckle as fast as the car would go, about 25 miles an hour, and up the 3rd hill out of Arbuckle we went and we made it. A few miles further on, we came to a paved road and we sailed into Erie without further mishap as dust settled over the city.

Faye Armstrong, my best friend Clive's mother, had told me that after I lived in a big city like Erie, I would never want to live in a little country village like Chapmansville again. I told her this was not true. But, she was right. We never moved back to Chapmansville.

The Yellow Road

In 1950, we lived in a rented house in Brookhaven, a suburb of Chester, Pennsylvania. In June of that year, we bought a house a few miles away in Springfield, a suburb of Philadelphia. Prior to moving into our new house, which we could not do until the end of August, my wife and I decided to make a trip to our hometown Erie, Pennsylvania to visit our mothers and our brothers and sisters. This we routinely did at least once a year, and sometimes more often. We decided also, that after visiting our relatives, we would take the children on a trip though Canada and back through New England. At the time, my daughter Bonnie Lee was just 11 years old, and my son Richard was just a month short of five.

After spending several days visiting our relatives, we started on our trip through Canada. In Erie, we had learned that our church denomination was holding a Young People's Convention in Toronto, and we decided to stop at the convention for a couple of hours in order to meet some friends of long standing whom we had not seen for several years. Other than that, we would plan our trip as we went along.

Our first stop was at Niagara Falls, which neither Bonnie Lee, nor Richard had seen before. We went over the Peace Bridge at Buffalo into Canada and on to the Canadian side of the falls, which are far more spectacular than the American falls. We spent several hours watching the falls, and by the time we got to Toronto it was late in the evening. We had a problem getting a hotel, and settled for a small hotel over a saloon. The proprietor, it seemed to me, was somewhat hesitant to rent the room to us. I wondered later that perhaps he was in the habit generally of renting his rooms for 'one night stands', not to tourists.

After breakfast the next day, we went to the church where the convention was being held and attended the morning service where we met some of the friends we had been anxious to see. At the close of the service, we continued on our way. The road from Toronto to Montreal and to Quebec City was called the Kings Highway. It was a four-lane road. I remarked to a gas station attendant about how nice this Canadian road was and he laughed and said, "Yes, the Kings Highway is a nice road, but it is the only such road in Canada."

A couple of hours after we left Toronto, we arrived at the end of Lake Ontario where the St. Lawrence River begins. At the beginning of the river, there are what are called the Thousand Islands. We took a boat ride though these islands. One of them was owned by Arthur Godfrey, a television personality at the time whom my children watched each week. They were very excited about seeing Arthur Godfrey's Island.

After the boat ride, we proceeded along the Kings Highway for a few miles and then turned left on a highway that led to Ottawa, the capital of Canada. We went through the Capitol Building, including going to the top of the tower. Ottawa was not a large city at the time, and looking from the tower, their seemed to be nothing but wilderness north of the city.

After visiting the Capitol Building, we drove south back to the Kings Highway and turned towards Montreal. By this time, it was getting late and we started looking for a place to stay for the night. Nights in Canada, in August, are cool and all the signs for cabins emphasized 'heated cabins'.

When we rented a cabin, we found that the heat was provided by little wood stoves. We were provided with a little pile of wood. We, of course, were required to start the fire in the stove and keep it going ourselves.

The next morning we proceeded on the Kings Highway to
Montreal. We drove into the center of the city. We thought it
to be an attractive city, but we didn't stay long. We continued
on to Quebec City, which is built on a bluff overlooking the
St. Lawrence River. I had always wanted to see the Plains of
Abraham where General Wolfe was killed in the French and
Indian War. General Wolfe, by nature, was more of a poet than
a soldier. He once said he would rather have written the poem,
Grey's Elegy, than to have won a battle. The location of the
battlefield has been made into a beautiful park. I hired a guide,
and we took a tour of the city. Quebec City seemed to me to be a
typical French city and very attractive in its architecture.

At the completion of our tour of Quebec City, we crossed the
St. Lawrence and headed back to the United States. It was getting
late and after crossing the St. Lawrence, we quickly found another
'heated cabin' with its little wood stove. The next day, driving
though Quebec Province, we went though many small towns and
villages. The most prominent buildings in each of these places were
large steepled churches. The French Canadians who lived there are
mostly devout Catholics. The social life in these towns, I thought,
probably largely revolves around these churches, much like it did in
the small Protestant Pennsylvania village where I was born.

We crossed into the United States into Vermont, and
then quickly turned left into New Hampshire and to Mount
Washington. There was a small train, which would have taken
us to the top of Mount Washington, but this would have taken
several hours. It was getting late in the afternoon so we didn't
take it, which I have always regretted. We proceeded on into
Maine. Motels were scarce at the time, but we found a tourist
home, not far from Portland, where we spent the night.

The next morning, we drove into Portland. In Portland, I saw ahead of me, in traffic, a red Ford convertible with a black top. A friend of mine, who lived in Washington, had such a car. He had come from the Portland, Maine area. I said to Alice, "That looks like Ernie's car. Maybe Ernie is visiting his hometown on vacation." I tried to catch up with the red convertible, but lost it in traffic. Afterwards, I checked with Ernie, but he said he wasn't in Portland at the time.

We proceeded from Portland through New Hampshire into Massachusetts and into Boston. The only sightseeing we did in Boston was to go to the top of the Bunker Hill monument. From the top, we could look out over the city of Boston, which looks much different now than at the time of the Battle of Bunker Hill.

From Boston, we proceeded south to Plymouth. We wanted to see Plymouth Rock. My daughter Bonnie Lee was very disappointed with Plymouth Rock. She thought it would be much larger than it is. At Plymouth Rock, there was a teenage boy, dressed in a Pilgrim costume, who gave a little lecture about Plymouth Rock to the tourists gathered around. When he finished, he took his hat off and said, "I will now take up a collection for my own benefit."

From Plymouth Rock, we drove on through Providence, Rhode Island into Connecticut and to New Haven, where we stayed overnight with a boyhood friend and his family who had moved to New Haven from Erie. That evening, we took a tour of Yale University. On the final day of our trip, we drove back through Philadelphia to Brookhaven for the final two weeks before we moved into our new home in Scenic Hills.

Before I started the trip, I had the 3A's mark out a route on one of their maps. They used a heavy yellow pencil. All during the trip, Bonnie Lee and Richard kept asking me if we were still on the "Yellow Road."

Thought For The Day

This brief essay was delivered to the writer's group at Lighthouse Point, Florida on May 8, 2001.

Niels Bohr, the physicist and Nobel Prize winner who discovered that the uranium atom, when split, could produce a power millions of times greater than anything known on earth, kept a horse shoe over the door of his house in Denmark. He was asked if he believed in luck. He said, "No, but sometimes it helps even if you don't believe in it."

Like Bohr, I have never believed in luck. If offered a rabbit foot to carry for luck, my position would be that it didn't bring luck to the rabbit, so why would it bring luck to me.

But as Bohr noted, luck sometimes comes even if you don't believe in it. It was just luck that I heard about the start of a writers group in Bowie and it was just luck that Mary Paneton told me about this group. I feel very fortunate, through these groups, to have met so many talented and nice people. I enjoy the writers group meetings very much.

This is my last day with you all for a while. I plan on leaving for Maryland on Friday; God willing, I'll see you all in the fall.

[Editor's note: The author returned to Pompano Beach in the fall of 2002 and returned to the group at Lighthouse Point for one final season. He drove himself and his wife Alice in a new automobile. He was 89 at the time and turned 90 a few days later. This trip to Florida was the last time that he drove there.]

A Walk in the Snow

*This essay was written in October 2002 and delivered first to the
Bowie Senior Writers' group.*

I was brought up Erie, Pennsylvania, known as the Gem
City. In 1925, when my twin brother Roy and I were 12 years
old, we moved to Franklin Park, a settlement of small brick row
houses just inside the eastern boundary of Erie. To the south,
about a block away, ran the main tracks of the New York Central
Railroad. A couple of blocks south of the railroad tracks ran
Buffalo Road, Route 20, the main road between Cleveland, Ohio
and Buffalo, New York. To the east of Erie, there were fields and
woods and creeks. Depending on their distance from the center
of Erie, the creeks were called Four Mile Creek, Five Mile Creek,
Six Mile Creek, and so forth. To the west between Franklin Park
and the built-up part of Erie, about three-fourths of a mile, were
fields and woods and numerous small swamps. These swamps
contained muskrats, which Roy and I trapped during the winter
months.

During school days, Roy and I would set our traps around
Franklin Park, but on weekends we would go to the creeks east
of Erie, generally Six Mile Creek, and set our traps in that area.
We would go out to Six Mile Creek on Saturday and set our
traps, and then on Sunday go back and pick them up. We were
generally joined on weekends by our friend, Walt Fuhrman.
Walt lived in the center of Erie about two and a half miles from
Franklin Park. Walt was 16 years old in July 1925. At that time,
he quit school. He trapped in the wintertime when he was unable
to find other work.

Thanksgiving holidays gave us an opportunity to trap around

Six Mile Creek for several days in a row. Over Thanksgiving 1927, we went out to that area every day during the period from Thursday through Sunday. On Sunday, when we would have ordinarily picked up our traps, we decided that we would leave them there one more day and go out after school on Monday to pick them up.

Walt met us when school left out at 2:30 p.m. on Monday. It had been snowing lightly all day, but there was only an inch or two of light fluffy snow on the ground when we got out of school. We walked the one quarter of a mile home from the school where Roy and I put on our rubber boots, which we would need

Walt Fuhrman was Ray's beloved child-hood friend and trapping partner.

for wading around in Six Mile Creek. By 3:30 p.m., we were on our way.

We did not dally in our walk, and by 4:30 p.m., we were in the woods around the Six Mile Creek. The snow was getting heavier, and by this time, there were four or five inches of snow on the ground. The woods around Six Mile Creek extended east for a couple of miles. We had set some traps about half a mile east of Six Mile Creek at a little brook we called Mink Creek. We called it Mink Creek because we had once seen mink tracks there. After picking up our traps at Six Mile Creek, we went through the woods and across a dirt road and on into the woods on the other side. From the road, it was about a quarter of a mile to Mink Creek. By the time we had picked up our traps, it was starting to get dark.

We couldn't see very far but we knew exactly where we were.

Walt said, "We better get back to that road before the tracks we made coming in here get covered up and we can't find our way back."

We knew that we had to get back to the dirt road we had crossed. At this point, we hurried as fast as we could. It was now snowing very hard.

When we reached the dirt road, we were still in the middle of nowhere, three and a half miles from home. Not a light anywhere. It was about 6 p.m. and completely dark. It was snowing harder than ever, with eight inches of snow on the ground. We couldn't go back the way we came with short cuts through fields and woods. We had to stick to the roads. We had several options. Walt said we ought to go back by the Buffalo Road. Roy and I thought we ought to go home by another road, the Harbor Creek Road, because it was a little closer home that way.

Walt said, "There is a street car that comes out on the Buffalo Road about a mile west of Six Mile Creek." This was about a mile and a half from where we then were. Roy and I told Walt we didn't have any money. "I only have a dime," Walt said.

While we were having this discussion, we were walking up the dirt road through the snow, which was getting deeper by the minute. We stayed as close together as possible. In the snow and darkness we didn't want to lose contact with each other. The dirt road ended on Harbor Creek Road. Here a decision had to be made. Would we turn west on Harbor Creek Road or would we cross about 100 yards of open field, climb over the railroad tracks and then over another field to Buffalo Road. I told Walt it would be dangerous going over the railroad tracks because we couldn't see if a train was coming because of the snow. Walt said you can hear a humming on the tracks if a train is coming.

Roy and I didn't want Walt to go by himself, so we decided to go to the Buffalo Road with him. We waded through what was now about a foot of snow to the railroad tracks. We listened carefully, but could hear no humming, so we scurried over the tracks as fast as we could go. In a few minutes, we were on Buffalo Road. It was now 7 p.m. It was snowing heavier than ever. We could barely see the road. There were no auto tracks in the road even though it was a main thoroughfare. Nobody was on the roads because of the blizzard.

By this time, we were getting very tired. We had walked six miles in the snow since leaving school, and we still had three and a half miles to go. A wind had come up and we would have to face it the rest of the way home. In addition to being very tired, we were cold and hungry. We had had nothing to eat since lunch. The temperature had fallen to 20 degrees.

Because of the heavy snow, it took us over an hour to walk the mile down Buffalo Road to where the street car was supposed to come. We were surprised when we got there to see it waiting. Walt now had it made. He had a dime. He could ride in comfort the nearly four and a half miles to his home. Roy and I had nearly two and a half miles yet to go through the snow. We stood there as Walt got on the streetcar and dropped his dime in the moneybox. There was nobody else on the streetcar. The dour-looking motorman looked at Roy and me. "Are you getting on?" he asked.

"We don't have any money," Roy said.

The motorman looked at the heavily falling snow. He looked at the two small boys standing there. I was five feet one inch and weighed just 100 pounds at the time. Roy was slightly larger.

"Where do you live?" he said.

"Franklin Park," we replied.

His streetcar went about half a mile from Franklin Park. Grumpily, he said, "Get on." He was a more kindhearted man than he looked.

Roy and I got on the streetcar as fast as we could before the motorman could change his mind. He let us off at the street that led to Franklin Park. By this time, we had warmed up in the nice warm streetcar. We had no problem the rest of the way home. I don't remember whether either Roy or I said thank you to the motorman. Probably not.

About Dogs and Cats and Other Things

My twin brother Roy and I were born in 1912 on a farm near the village of Chapmansville in northwestern Pennsylvania. My family moved quite often while we were growing up. When we were 18 months old, we moved to a house near Franklin, Pennsylvania, and when 7 years old, back to Chapmansville. When 10 years old, we moved to Erie, Pennsylvania, where we eventually ended up in Franklin Park, the location of many of my short stories. Our best friend while we were growing up in Franklin Park was Walt Fuhrman.

Chapmansville was named for John Chapman. He may well have been the John Chapman who is better known to history as Johnny Appleseed. In the first part of the 19th century, Johnny Appleseed wandered around western Pennsylvania and eastern Ohio planting apple orchards. According to family tradition, my mother's ancestors, consisting of Great-Great-Aunt Emily and her stodgy husband, Great-Great-Uncle Elmer, moved to western Pennsylvania about 1810. Also according to family tradition, Aunt Emily was a very lively lady and didn't let stodgy Uncle Elmer hold her back. I have often wondered whether she had seduced Johnny Appleseed, of course unbeknown to Stodgy Uncle Elmer, and that the genes I received four generations later from this relationship is the reason I have always been so fond of apples.

But to get back to the subject of this essay, Dogs and Cats and Other things. As I was growing up, our family never owned a dog. Cats we had, but never a dog. Other than cats, the only other pets we had were a crow and guinea pigs. Although never owing a dog ourselves, I remember several dogs owned by friends or relatives, and in a couple of cases, strays.

The pet crow we had belonged to Roy. One day while on a hike into the woods with Walt Fuhrman, Roy had climbed to the top of a tree and taken the crow out of its nest when it was half grown. We kept the crow outside in a tree. We fed it bread and water, which went through him or her like a sieve. The tree and yard were soon a mess. After several weeks, it came up missing. We never knew what happened to it. It may have flown away, although Roy kept its wings chipped to prevent this. It could have succumbed to a predator or it could have been stolen. A woman passing the house once tried to buy the crow from Roy.

We kept the guinea pigs in the attic where Roy and I slept. One cold night, they froze to death.

After we moved to Erie, my brother and I, for several years, spent weeks each summer with my Uncle Bill who lived on a farm near Chapmansville. Uncle Bill had a dog that he kept tied up in his side yard.

One night, a stray dog came into the yard. The farmers around Chapmansville didn't approve of dogs running loose especially at night. They feared they would kill sheep. My uncle aroused my older cousin, about 10 years older than me, and he opened the window in the room where my younger cousin and I were sleeping and shot the stray. The shot did not awaken me but the talking afterwards of my uncle, aunt and cousin did. My younger cousin did not waken during the whole commotion. I wish I could sleep that soundly now.

Sleeping with my cousin reminds me of a somewhat risqué story, which I guess I shouldn't tell. Oh well, you are a mature audience, so I will tell it anyway. As the story goes, the city boy went to visit his country cousin. When they went to bed that night, the city boy, after jumping in bed, noticed that his country cousin was kneeling by the side of the bed with his head down.

When he saw this he thought, *maybe I should say my prayers too.*
So, he got out the other side of the bed and kneeled down. At
this, his country cousin looked up and said, "Ma's going to be
really mad at you. The pot is on this side of the bed."

In Franklin Park, several families had dogs, which they
generally kept tied up or at least on their own property. At
one time, however, the area became overrun with strays, which
nobody seemed to own. One of them was a small female brown
dog, which my family fed from time to time, but never took
ownership of. We called her Brownie. Brownie would go with
Roy and me and our friend Walt when we went on hikes into
the country and the woods. Brownie was a spunky little dog.
She once tackled a woodchuck almost as big as herself. She was
not able to handle the woodchuck, and it got away. One day, the
caretaker of Franklin Park rounded up all the stray dogs running
around and destroyed them, including Brownie. My father said
after this happened that he wished he had taken Brownie in and
gotten her a license, but it was too late. Brownie was the closest
we came to having a dog of our own when we were growing up.

We got our first cat when we lived near Franklin. It was
a black female cat that followed Roy home from school.
Nobody claimed her, and a year later when we moved back to
Chapmansville, we took her with us. This cat once had a litter
of kittens in my Dad's bed. He felt the cat and the kittens with
his bare foot when he went to bed. When we moved to Erie,
Dad gave this cat to a farmer who lived far enough away from
Chapmansville so that it was unlikely to find its way back to our
house.

One winter day when coming home from looking at my
muskrat traps, I noticed a mother cat and kitten who seemed
to want to stay close to me. They followed me home much like

the black cat that followed Roy home from school. I admit that I walked as slow as I could. My father said we could keep them. The kitten came up missing a few days later, but the old cat stayed around for several years. It had two litters of kittens before, it too, came up missing. The world is a dangerous place for cats that are allowed to roam around outside at night.

I don't remember what happened to the kittens except for one we called Lindy. When grown, Lindy was a good-sized, tiger-colored cat. Lindy came up missing for a week when he was about 2 years old. Just by chance, I went into a vacant house a couple of doors away and there was Lindy. He could hardly stand he was so weak from hunger and thirst. Lindy was never healthy after this, and finally it was decided to destroy him. Roy put him in a basket and went out into the woods where he was going to shoot him. While digging a hole to bury him, Lindy got away and came back home. I do not remember what was Lindy's eventual end, but Roy made no further attempt to destroy him at the time.

Our friend Walt had a little dog named Jack, mostly fox terrier. Walt sometimes brought Jack along with us on our hikes. Jack was afraid of a loud noise. Once, when we were out in the country about five or six miles from where Walt lived in the center of Erie, a gun was shot off and Jack immediately scooted for home. He made it safely. One time, we sicked Jack on a cat we saw in a field by the side of the road and he, with a yelp, tore after it as fast as he could go. The cat jumped on his back and dug his claws into him and Jack came yelping back to us at even a faster pace than he had left. The cat jumped off his back before he got back to us and ran back into the field, or we would probably have ran ourselves. Jack developed a phobia for cats after this.

Well, so much for the dogs, cats and other pets in my life when I was growing up. After I married and left home, I didn't get a dog until I got one for my daughter, Bonnie, when she was 12 years old. We never had a cat. When Bonnie got married and left home, Tippy became my dog, the only dog I have ever owned. She has been dead for 38 years, enjoying, I am sure, the blessings of dog heaven. She was a sweet dog. I still carry a picture of her in my wallet.

Adversity

Sweet are the uses of adversity, which like the toad, ugly and venomous, wears yet a precious jewel in his head. Thus said the old Duke in Shakespeare's *As You The Like It* as he wandered round in the forest of Arden where he was living in banishment after his younger brother usurped his Dukedom. The old Duke was wrong biologically about the toad but he had a point about adversity at least as it has been with me.

When I graduated from high school in January 1931, we were in the depth of the Great Depression. Through good fortune I obtained a job as mail boy at the General Telephone Company in Erie, Pennsylvania. My entrance salary was $12.00 per week. After a year I was moved to the addressograph department where I worked for 5 1/2 years. Raises in pay were infrequent and when I finally found another job and left the telephone company in 1937, I was receiving $18.00 a week.

I was ambitious and tried to prepare myself for a better position. I had no hope of going to college so I went to night school in Erie and studied accounting. I hoped to get a job in the accounting department. I asked the treasurer for such a job but he never gave me one. At the time he could hire recent graduates from accounting schools at a minimum salary. Probably he thought that he would gain nothing by transferring me to the accounting department and might have trouble in getting somebody who would do as well as I was doing in the job I had. The general opinion among telephone company underlings was that the treasurer had little concern for anybody but himself.

If I had been transferred to the accounting department, I probably would have spent my entire working life at the telephone company. I would have worked my whole life in a routine job. I didn't feel this way at the time, but I now thank God he didn't transfer me.

Not being able to have the career I envisioned in the telephone company I sought opportunities elsewhere. This was not easy to do in Erie during the Depression. Jobs of any kind were hard to find. In 1937 I saw a notice in the Post Office relative to a U. S. Government examination for accounting clerks. I applied and took the examination, which I succeeded in passing. I was on the career civil service list for several years. Meanwhile I finally found another routine job but one that paid somewhat more than I was receiving at the telephone company. I received three offers of short-term appointments to the government of which I took only one at a time when I was temporarily out of work.

Eventually with the defense buildup in 1940 I received a permanent appointment with the Department of War (now the Department of Defense) in Philadelphia and moved away from Erie. During the following 32 years I worked for several government agencies. When I worked for the General Accounting Office pressure was put on the staff to become Certified Public Accountants. I studied for the examination and became a CPA. During the last twenty years of my government service I was in a position of authority where I traveled extensively not only in the United States but in Europe and the Far East. My job was very interesting and fulfilling as well.

I often think, "What if the treasurer of the telephone company had been a nice guy, acceded to my desire at the time and transferred me to the accounting department." If so, I would never have had such an interesting and fulfilling career. I would never have seen so much of the world. I would never have moved to Bowie and met all you nice people. I hear somebody saying,

"Flattery will get you nowhere."

Sometimes in the beginning we can have dreams that we wonder if we will ever realize. In my case my dreams all came true.

Anniversary

Delivered to the Bowie Senior Writers' Group on September 12, 2000.

Mathematicians have estimated that if a chimpanzee pounded away at a typewriter and did it a sufficient number of times that eventually he or she would come up with *Hamlet* or its equivalent. No estimate has been made, as far as I know, as to how many times the chimpanzee would have to pound away to get this result. It probably would be something like a trillion, trillion, trillion times, or maybe more.

Six years ago this month eight humans, the next evolutionary level above chimpanzees, met in Bowie City Hall to start the Bowie Senior Writers' Group. Using an average of 6 new articles read by its members each week I estimate that the group has produced 1,800 articles over the past six years. Like our evolutionary predecessors none of us has produced anything equal to *Hamlet* yet. Yet. But with few exceptions what has been produced and read at our meetings has been interesting. And every once in a while there has been, like Art Ackerman's "Edna," a gem produced. You can read 18 of these gems on the seniors' web site. But there were many more.

When I went to that first meeting on that September Tuesday six years ago, I was apprehensive that I was getting in over my head. I felt that people who would join such a group would be far better educated than I and far better writers than I could ever hope to be. This proved to be true. Nevertheless I was accepted by the group and, on the one or two occasions when I surpassed myself, they even seemed to enjoy what I had written.

After I returned to Florida that fall, Mary Panneton called me and invited me to a Writers' Group that she attended during the winter months at Lighthouse Point, Florida. At the time the group had between 15 and 18 members. It was a much younger group and much more interested in getting something published than my Bowie group. Looking at me, an old man 84 years old, I could see they expected little from me except perhaps to waste their time. I was informed at my first meeting that they had a rule you had to attend the meetings for a month before you would be permitted to read anything. When the next week, not discouraged, I returned. I was informed that they were grandfathering me in and that I could read something I had written if I cared to. At first I did not feel accepted in the group but over the years I believe I have wormed myself into their affection.

Joining the two writers' groups has been the best thing that happened to me in my eighties. New friends have been made that has enriched my old age. Instead of dozing before the television set I am keeping my remaining brain cells active because of a desire to have something new to read to the groups each Tuesday. I have even gotten on the Internet and I am now taking advantage of the technical advances of the last few years. Without the writers groups I would never have done this.

The prophet Joel said, "Young men see visions, old men dream dreams." Because of the writers groups I attend, I have been made to realize that although I am full of years it is still possible for me to see visions. I need not be content to dream away my remaining years.

Visit To Vietnam

In 1969, I made a trip to Vietnam. It had come to the attention of the Department of the Army that the sergeants who ran the NCO (Noncommissioned Officers) Clubs, particularly in overseas areas, were skimming off receipts from bar sales and slot machines. I was assigned to make a survey of the situation and to make a recommendation as to what measures should be taken to correct the situation and to prevent this from happening in the future.

To you who are not familiar with how the clubs the army maintains operate, I will note that there are two separate systems, one for the officers clubs and a separate one for enlisted personal. Each club operates as a separate entity with the club manager responsible only to his commanding officer. There appeared to be no problem with the officers clubs; only with the NCO clubs. The managers of the officers clubs were generally low grade officers, that is lieutenants and captains. The NCO clubs were generally managed by sergeants who were derisively referred to, at least by the draftees, as "Lifers," that is, enlisted personnel who had stayed in the army for a career.

I arrived in Saigon, Vietnam on November 14. On the way, I stopped in Honolulu, Japan, Korea and Okinawa. At each of these locations I visited NCO clubs, talked with the people in charge, and reviewed fiscal and operational procedures.

The Army Audit Agency, for whom I worked, had an area office in Saigon with two people assigned to it. The auditor in charge Bob Shankin assigned his assistant, Nick Hoggendyck, to assist me. Nick was assigned to accompany me throughout my visit to Vietnam.

My first visit, after I arrived in Saigon, was to Long Bein

about 20 miles north of Saigon. Long Bein was the headquarters of the U. S. Army in Vietnam. At Long Bein, I spoke with the comptroller, who was a full colonel and made arrangements for me to visit selected NCO clubs. My first visit was to an NCO club near what was called, The Eagles Peak, not far from Cambodia. Hoggendyck and I were given a bubble top helicopter to get there. The pilot was a young GI. I was sitting by the open door and never did find out how to fasten the seat belt. I was lucky not to fall out.

I met with the officer who was in charge of the club. The club had a defalcation of nearly $100,000. The officer claimed a Chinese bookkeeper had disappeared with the money. He claimed he couldn't get American bookkeepers. I asked him why he didn't use enlisted draftees, who had an accounting education. He said the commanding officer thought the draftees should take their lumps as he expressed it. I saw the CO when I went back to my helicopter to go back to Long Bein. He was getting off his helicopter with a big cigar in his mouth with his assistants fluttering around him.

A couple of days later the comptroller assigned me a major and an lieutenant to accompany Hoggendyck and me to Bam Me Thuot in the central highlands about 200 miles from Saigon. Bam Me Thuot was supposed to be pacified at the time. We left in a small two motored plane from Ben Huo, an air base about 10 miles from Long Bein. All the way to Bam Me Thuot I could see a steady stream of bomb craters on the mountain sides and in the rice paddies. We landed in an unpaved airfield.

While waiting for a car, I noticed a group of young GI's waiting for a helicopter to take them out in the jungle where they could wander around for a week or so looking for Vietcong, whom they could kill or get killed by. The genius who invented this type of operation accomplished little except to get a lot of American kids killed or maimed. I didn't see anyone in the group who looked over 20 years old. Lifers, career enlisted personnel, were too smart to get assigned to such an operation. The Lifers sent to Vietnam generally got safe jobs back in Long Bein.

At Bam Me Thuot, I visited the Officers Club and a closed NCO Club. The Officers Club was fully operative. It had in the past taken a shell hit, which made a big hole in the floor and blown the roof off. But, the hole had been filled in and cemented over and the roof repaired. The NCO Club had been closed for several months. For recreation, the GI's went to a club like set up operated at a Chinese laundry.

The major told me the reason the NCO Club was closed was that the sergeant who was in charge had cleaned out the till. I asked what had happened to him. The major said he had been transferred to Da Nang and then back to the States. I told the major that I bet he got a medal to take back to the States with him. The major did not deny this. When I got back to Long Bein, I told the comptroller that it wouldn't look good in my report that they couldn't reopen the NCO Club in Bam Me Thuot while the Officers Club was operating full blast. A couple of weeks after I returned to Washington, I got a letter from Hoggendyck. He said Command had sent somebody to Bam Me Thuot and reopened the NCO Club. My trip wasn't entirely useless.

After checking out the two clubs in Bam Me Thuot. Hoggendyck and I were assigned a jeep with a driver and a GI rode shotgun. We went about seven miles down into the jungle to an engineering unit which was pulling out. This unit had a small NCO club. It is noted that the U. S. Army was just starting to pull out of Vietnam at this time, a process, which would take five years. I was a little nervous about this trip into the jungle but nothing happened.

During the nights in Saigon, I could hear guns going off every once in a while, which was probably just nervous Republic of Vietnam Army soldiers. At the camp near the Eagles Peak I heard outgoing cannon fire in the distance but nothing coming in. I couldn't tell whether the Vietnamese I saw were Vietcong or the Vietnamese on our side. They all looked mad. After I visited Vietnam, I had no doubt in my mind that we had no business there and never had had.

While I was in Saigon, I took a tour of the city. I visited the Chinese business section that had been devastated during the Tet offensive. It was in full operation. The presidential palace was completely surrounded by barbed wire as were many other buildings in Saigon. The American Embassy was surrounded by a high fence and also by barbed wire. I saw a movie once where William Holden had dinner with his lady friend at a crowded luxurious boat restaurant on the Saigon River. I visited this boat. It was actually a small, dirty spoon type of boat restaurant with few customers. The war had been going on for more than ten years, but there were still expensive French restaurants in Saigon.

It was found that the top sergeant of the Army, a position equivalent to the Chief of Staff, was involved in the NCO club scandal. Neither he or any of the other sergeants involved were ever prosecuted. In my opinion, they all had too much on the generals. As a result of my review, periodic audits of the clubs were started which at least would bring to light instances of fraud in the Army Officer and NCO Clubs before they became an army wide scandal.

The War On Terrorism
(What I Really Think)

A young would be entrepreneur was once advised that if he wanted to be sure to succeed in business he should make and sell a product that:

1. Everybody has to have,
2. That nobody else could provide except himself, and
3. That wore out quickly.

The American military was in this inevitable position for over forty-five years. There stood the dear, old Soviet Union an obvious threat to everything we hold dear. No one could protect the free world from the Soviet Union and communism except the American military. Such a menace could justify the ever increasing expenditures year after year. Money for more billion dollar aircraft carriers, money for star wars, money for the large producers of military equipment, money for more General and Admiral slots in the military hierarchy were made readily available. No one in the military industrial complex, which General Eisenhower warned us about, dreamed that this favorable situation would ever end.

At budget preparation time it didn't hurt to remind the American public of the Communist threat. At such times problems in Taiwan or Quonoy or the Chinese threat would be brought to the attention of the American public or it would be alleged that North Korea or Hungary or Poland had become danger spots. The budget would be passed and we would hear no more about Taiwan or Quonoy or the other danger spots until the next budget preparation period at which time these problems would flair up again.

Then, horror of horror, the Soviet Union collapsed. The Berlin wall came tumbling down. Germany reunited. Poland and the other Soviet dominated countries became democracies. China became more interested in selling cheap goods to the United States than in opposing us. To say that panic struck the military industrial complex is to minimize the effect all of this had. Their fears were well founded. Congress began cutting down the military budgets and closing useless bases both at home and overseas.

What to do? There seemed to be no threat anywhere justifying a large growing military force with a need to have its equipment modernized periodically. Going into Panama and arresting and putting Noriga in jail didn't seem to do the trick. Actually, this action was counterproductive as Noriga in jail was no longer a threat justifying large military forces in the Canal Zone. The Gulf War provided a temporary respite. But, it didn't last even through we let Saddam remain in Baghdad, where he could still be considered a danger to all we held sacred. Later, we went into Bosnia and into Kosovo. These were minor excursions and did little to halt the down sizing of the military. There was some talk of uniting Korea. North Korea for a time seemed interested. This would have eliminated the need for the thirty thousand American troops in Korea. We have not heard anything about uniting Korea recently. Do we need to wonder why?

The American people and Congress, and even the President, became interested in education, social security, Medicare, and the environment. Only lip service was being given to the military. From the viewpoint of the military, times were becoming desperate. But, the devil takes care of his own. Some Muslim religious fanatics hi-jacked some airliners and blew up the New York Trade Center and part of the Pentagon.

The rejoicing in Congress and at the White House was

hidden behind dour countenances. A war on terrorism was declared and Congress and the President had no need to worry anymore about the real problems facing the country. Wars previously declared against crime and drugs had attracted little notice and little results but a war against terrorism was something else. All the non-criminals and nondrug users in the country could see the results of terrorism on the nightly news and worry about how it might affect them personally. You can imagine the jubilance in the higher elements of the Pentagon. Terrorists, like the poor, we will always have with us. Military budgets will never again be a problem.

Immediately after the bombing of the World Trade Center and the Pentagon, a cry went out by the ignorant to bomb the hell out of them though nobody knew who "them" were. Big Oil who had financed the election of the administration and much of Congress saw its chance. They, ever since the blowup of the Soviet Union, had wanted to tap the oil reserves around the Caspian Sea. These reserves, I have read, are the largest in the world even exceeding the reserves around the Persian Gulf. But there is a problem getting the oil to market. The solution is to build pipelines similar to those in Alaska. The most practical way to go with these pipelines is through Afghanistan and either through Pakistan or though a corner of Iran or Iraq to the Arabian Sea or the Persian Gulf. Apparently, political problems and the terrain makes it impractical to build pipelines to a Black Sea port, or perhaps this would involve Russia too much for our liking.

Although fifteen of the September 11 bombers were Saudi Arabians, we couldn't bomb the Saudis with all their oil. The reason for selecting Afghanistan to "Bomb the hell out of" is self-evident. Its government was disorganized and militarily weak. An excuse was ready at hand. Although none of the terrorists involved in the bombings were Afghanis, it was alleged they belonged to a group that trained in Afghanistan. The real reason was that Afghanistan is close to the Caspian oil fields. Bombing Afghanistan gave us an excuse to build a large airfield in Ubekistran, which when completed will house 4,000 military personnel. This airfield will serve as a base for exploiting the Caspian Oil fields and protecting American interests there.

There have always been terrorists and there always will be. Nothing done today will eliminate them or even reduce their numbers substantially. For 300 years, the wild Indians were the terrorists we had to worry about. We finally killed most of them off and tamed the rest. We have always had criminals who are not much different than what we today call terrorists. We have over a million of them locked up with little noticeable improvement in public safety. Criminals, like today's alleged terrorists, have often been well organized and probably are today. Today's war on terror, in my opinion, is nothing but a cover up for the activities of big oil and the politicians who depend on funds they receive from the oil barons for use in their reelection.

Declaration of Independence

Delivered to the Bowie Senior Writer's Group on July 11, 2000.

A week ago, we celebrated what we called, when I was young, the 4th of July, the day the Declaration of Independence was signed. In these latter years we call this Independence Day. Actual independence did not come, however, for seven long years after the signing and only after a hard fought war in which victory was in doubt until the very end.

Have you ever wondered what kind of men the fifty-six signers were? Twenty-four were lawyers and jurists. Eleven were merchants; nine were farmers and large plantation owners. These men were not wild-eyed, rabble-rousing ruffians. They, for the most part, were men of means and education. They had security and status, but they valued liberty more.

We were British subjects at the time and we were fighting our own government. These men signed the Declaration of Independence knowing full well what would happen to them if the British captured them during the war or if in the end the war for independence was unsuccessful. When they pledged to each other their lives, their fortunes, and their sacred honor these were not idle words.

The history books tell us little of what happened to these men during the war, which followed the signing. Most paid a high price for their patriotism.

Five signers were captured by the British as traitors and tortured before they died.

Nine of the fifty-six fought and died from their wounds or hardships during the war.

Twelve had their homes ransacked and burned. Two lost sons serving in the Revolutionary Army. Another two had their sons captured.

Vandals or soldiers looted the properties of Dillery, Hall, Clymer, Walton, Gwinett, Heyward, Rutledge, and Middleton.

Carter Braxton of Virginia, a wealthy planter and trader, saw his ships swept from the seas by the British Navy. He sold his home and properties to pay his debts and died in poverty.

Thomas McKeam was so hounded by the British that he was forced to move his family constantly. His possessions were taken from him and poverty was his reward.

Francis Lewis had his home and properties destroyed. The British jailed his wife, and she died within a few months.

John Hart was driven from his wife's bedside as she was dying. Their 13 children fled for their lives. His fields and gristmill were laid to waste. He found his wife dead and his children vanished. A few weeks later he died of exhaustion and a broken heart.

At the battle of Yorktown, Thomas Nelson, Jr. noted that the British General Cornwallis had taken over the Nelson home for his headquarters. He quietly urged General Washington to open fire. The home was destroyed and Nelson died bankrupt.

The above men and the others who signed the Declaration Of Independence with their compatriots gave us independence and freedom. It is altogether fitting, to paraphrase President Lincoln in the Gettysburg address, that while we enjoy our 4th of July holiday and watch the fireworks each year, we stop for a moment and reflect on the sacrifices that the 56 signers of The Declaration of Independence made.

I Know This Much is True: A Book Review

Read to the Bowie Writers' Group on August 8, 2000

I recently read Wally Lamb's 900 page novel, *I Know This Much is True.* The narrator of the story is Dominick Birdsey and the story evolves around Dominick's efforts to protect his schizophrenic identical twin brother, Thomas, from the problems he encounters as a result of Thomas' disease and the anger and guilt he feels because he is unsuccessful. Being an identical twin, Dominick also fears he will eventually succumb to the same disease as his brother.

Like much of today's literature the book is filled with profanity. The "F-word" and the "S-word" are used in almost every conversation, in fact in some conversations in almost every sentence. In no way does this add anything to the clarity of the discussions between the characters in the book. I have often wondered why present day authors, including this author, feel compelled to use such language so often. They must think that they are being more realistic. In my opinion they are wrong. Most people do not use such language in conversations with each other. With a few exceptions the people I have been associated with over the years have been able to express themselves without the use of such words. Most disturbing is that when authors use such language in their books, they legalize its use in ordinary conversation.

In spite of the language, the book is an absorbing one, especially for someone like myself who has a loved one who has fallen into the black hole of schizophrenia. I had difficulty in putting the book down.

The background story of the book is about the Dominick's

Sicilian grandfather, a cruel, self-centered, ambitious man, who immigrated from Sicily to Connecticut, the location of the story, when he was young. Just before he died, the grandfather wrote a history of his life and this story is intermingled with the story of Dominick. It is one reason why the book is so long.

In the first chapter, Thomas, who is on release from a mental institution, cuts off his hand. In his delusion, he thinks that by making this sacrifice, the publicity resulting will prevent President Bush and Saddam from starting the Gulf War. As a result of cutting off his hand, Thomas is placed in a full security mental institution. With many flashbacks to Dominick's and Thomas's childhood, the story proceeds from there.

The book has many well-developed and interesting characters. Some are cruel. Some are selfish. Some are stupid. Some all the foregoing. Dominick himself is far from lovable. An exception is Dr. Pavel, the caring Indian woman psychiatrist, who through her insight and kindness brings Dominick to a place where he can overcome his anger, begin to strengthen his relationships, and lead a reasonably happy life. The book's characters are a cross section of humanity.

The author's intermingling of characters and events must have required a lot of rearranging and rewriting. It must have required a lot of research and study. The author says in the acknowledgments that a novel of this size is both a big, shaggy beast and a complex process requiring faith, luck, moral support and knowledge far beyond what its author brings to it. He gives credit to a large number of people who helped him in its writing. The *St. Louis Post-Dispatch* said it is a work of astonishing craftsmanship, structural symmetry and literary self-awareness and indeed it is.

[Author's Note: After I read the above to the group many of the members took issue with my assertion that most people do not use the F. or S. words or other profanity in ordinary conversation. One member wanted to know if my hearing aid was working Ok. I received little or no support for my contention. Being kind people, none said 'old fogy' though perhaps I am.

Checking with my writer daughter later, I found that she supported the group's opinion and said I was wrong. Once I get my thoughts together I will write a rebuttal backing off a little but nevertheless defending my position.

I sent this review to the author Wally Lamb. He sent me a note, in his own handwriting, thanking me for my interest in his book and explaining his use of profanity. He also sent his best wishes to my writers' group.]

In Defense of Prudery

In my book review of Wally Lamb's novel, *I Know This Much Is True*, which I recently read to this group, I took issue with the language the author felt necessary to use in the conversations between the characters. I maintained that such language is not generally used by most people in actual conversations. I was surprised at the reaction I received. In the discussion that followed my reading, I was emphatically informed that I was wrong. Several told me that they themselves [*Did I detect a mite of braggadocio here?*] used such language on occasion. I would guess the occasions are infrequent. During the discussion, due to the kindness of the group, nobody said the words "old fogy" or "fuddy-duddy." I cannot deny that I am old, but I would have disputed an assertion that I was a "fogy" or a "fuddy-duddy." Checking with my writer daughter afterwards, she supported the group's opinion and said I was wrong about the use of profanity in this day and age.

Although I did not mention it in my review, there were also several explicit sexual encounters described in the book. In most instances the author was trying to relate the problems Dominick, the main character in the book, was having in his relations with the women in his life and to the emotional stress he was undergoing because of his schizophrenic twin brother. I felt he could have eliminated the specific detail of the encounters and still obtained the clarity he sought.

When Rhett Butler (Clark Gable) said, "I don't give a damn," in the movie *Gone With The Wind*, it caused endless comment by the media of the day. Some people were outraged. For others, it merely reinforced their belief that people would be better off if they and especially their children did not attend the movies.

When *Lady Chatterley's Lover* was published, it was banned as being pure pornography in certain places. It is noted that in this book it is only stated {maybe only hinted) that Lady Chatterley and the Gardener had sex. Little detail is included in the text. In today's atmosphere where the books we read, the movies and the television we watch are filled with explicit sex and I am told the language most people use in conversation is filled with profanity. We are only amused when we think of the way people thought and acted only a generation or two ago.

I was born in a farming community. When I was 10 years old we moved to a poor section of the city. The farmers and working men I grew up with used profanity regularly but not the kind we hear or read today. It was restricted mostly to "hell" or "damn." My father used such language on occasion. When he was angry, he used to say "damn it" or when especially angry "God Damn it!" He always ended his curse with 'it' never 'you'. I never heard my mother use a cuss word. When she was irritated she used to say, "Oh, Sugar." My aunt told me that my mother, when young, once slipped and said, "Oh, Shit," but I never heard this myself. The small farmers and the lower working class men I grew up with seldom used words with sexual connotations of any kind. Most wouldn't even say the word "pregnant." If they mentioned such a condition at all they would say, "She is going to have a baby," which was not said in front of children.

Farm children became aware of sex through observation of farm animals. City children did not have this advantage, but by their early teens most city children had picked up here and there enough information so that they knew about as much about sex as their country counterparts. Both knew little or nothing about human sexuality. Sources used to satisfy curiosity about the other sex and sex in general were pretty much limited to looking at the underwear ads in the Sears and Roebuck catalog or to reading excerpts from the Bible. The educated might have gotten their sexual titillations from Boccaccio's *The Decameron* or Tom Fielding's *Tom Jones,* but in Chapmansville where I was born or Franklin Park where I grew up, I doubt that anybody had ever heard of these two authors.

The Bible is full of sex. The Song of Solomon, completely sexual, contains some of the most beautiful love songs ever written, which was different from the so-called love songs of our rock driven generation. It was not until Adam and Eve were driven out of the Garden of Eden that they became aware of their sexuality. The writers of the Bible found it necessary to say only that Adam knew Eve. Present day novelists, catering to our macho generation, would have described in intimate detail the event from first awareness of sexuality to Adam telling Eve as they lie exhausted in the grass that he was glad she ate the apple.

Over my lifetime I have read thousands of books, as I am sure most of you have. There are so many books being written and published today that nobody could possibly read them all. But not to worry. You are missing nothing except perhaps a few hours of relaxation. With the possible exception of *Gone With The Wind,* I doubt that any novel written during my lifetime will be read by anybody a hundred years from now. To paraphrase a few words from *Macbeth,* they strut and fret an hour upon the stage and then are heard no more.

But then why should writers attempt to produce something that is truly nutritious to the mind when all the public wants is junk food?

Part Two: *Short Stories*

The Twins: Roy and Ray in their 70s still enjoying each other's company.

The Sage of Rainbow Lake

(A Spoof)

For many years my old friend Grandpa Stoops from Erie, Pennsylvania and I talked about fishing for rainbows at Rainbow Lake, which lies inland from Little Port Walters on Baranof Island in Southern Alaska.

We finally decided to make the trip in 1979. I contacted the Interior Department in Washington, D.C. where I was assured that the department maintained a fine corduroy path over the mountains from Little Port Walters to Rainbow Lake. I was told that although the lake was in the primeval Alaskan forest we should have no difficulty in reaching it. I also was told that we would be going into an uncharted wilderness and it was recommended, that for our own safety, we hire a couple of Indian guides to accompany us.

I telephoned Grandpa Stoops in Erie, Pennsylvania, reversing the charges, and told him what I had learned. We agreed that we would sneak away from our helpmates on July 19, 1979, and set out for Alaska for fulfillment of our life long dream.

After a hazardous journey by TWA and Alaska Airlines, we arrived in Juneau, Alaska, the capital of our 49th state. Grandpa Stoops gave me a couple of days to recuperate at the Red Dog Saloon while he hunted up a grizzled old bush pilot named Whiskers Brown who was happy to fly us to Little Port Walters in his old World War I plane, which he had fitted up with pontoons.

At Little Port Walters, we discussed our proposed trip to Rainbow Lake with the natives. They were of little help. They said that due to the hazards of the trip nobody from Little Port

Walters had visited Rainbow Lake for many years. Like the Interior Department in Washington, they recommended that we not undertake the trip without native guides who knew the country. After some searching, we finally found two Indians who reluctantly agreed, at our assurance of high wages, to serve as our guides. Their names were Tonto and Silverheels Stoops. I remarked to Grandpa Stoops at the similarity of last names. Grandpa Stoops was at a loss, at first, to account for this coincidence. Then he remembered, that according to family tradition, a great uncle had gone to Alaska many years before and had never been heard from again.

Sunrise broke over the heavy clouds that shrouded the beautiful Alaska waterland on July 22. Assembling our gear and our faithful Indian guides, Tonto and Silverheels, we set out for Rainbow Lake. The weather was typically Alaskan, raining like hell. Because of our exemplary lives, hell held no fear for us and neither did high water and so we started, up past the fish hatchery. We were soon in the untouched wilderness. The corduroy path described by the Interior Department in Washington was evident only part of the way and even in these parts were in sad repair. In fact, the corduroy path was one of the main hazards we were to encounter on our trip through the wilderness to Rainbow Lake.

But, to go on with my tale.

A short distance past the fish hatchery, the corduroy path largely disappeared and we had to depend entirely on our faithful Indian guides who indicated in sign language that they were following an old Indian trail that would take us to Rainbow Lake.

Grandpa Stoops and I would soon become somewhat disenchanted with our faithful Indian guides. They seemed to be chattering a lot in their native tongue. From time to time they would stop and point wildly in different directions. They would then take a piece of wampum and toss it into the air. They would look at the wampum where it fell and then would start out in the direction one of the guides had pointed. They would do this several times. After each toss they would take off, sometimes in the direction Tonto had pointed and then in the direction pointed out by Silverheels.

The rain continued to pour down. This made the rocks and the small sections of the remaining corduroy path very slippery. Several times I slipped and fell and Grandpa Stoops had to help me to my feet, which was especially difficult when our faithful Indian guide Silverheels had fallen on top of me. Battling the elements, the mud, the water, the dilapidated corduroy path, the high spruce trees that blocked the way, the slippery roots, the thick underbrush, the unending downpour, and my rain pants which were continually slipping down, we pressed on.

After what seemed several hours, we came to Jake's Canyon. Looking down we could barely see the raging torrent a hundred feet below. The only way across was by a forty-foot log, one foot in diameter, which stretched across the canyon. The Interior Department had strung a thin rope from a tree on each side of the canyon, which to hold while crossing. I looked aghast at the prospect before us.

I turned to Grandpa Stoops with tears in my eyes and said, "Grandpa Stoops, our dreams of fishing in Rainbow Lake are at an end. There is no way two silver beards our age can get across that narrow log bridge that spans the raging torrent below."

I looked at the Indian guides. I could see the scorn in their eyes at my fear of crossing the bridge. I turned again to Grandpa Stoops and said, "Do you see the scorn in the eyes of our faithful Indian guides?"

Grandpa Stoops replied, "We have no choice but to prove to our faithful Indian guides that we are not cowards. We must prove that intelligent, civilized, cultured men can face danger with the same fortitude as savages."

Grandpa Stoops hesitated but a moment. "Let's go," he said courageously. "We will cross together. If one slips the other can hold him up. We will show these savages, our faithful Indian guides, how civilized men face danger and survive."

Grasping the thin rope strung across the canyon, Grandpa Stoops started across with me trembling but close behind. Slowly we edged across the log bridge, which was swaying over the torrent, which raged below. With superhuman effort, we managed to maintain our balance until we were halfway across.

At this point, Grandpa Stoops decided to take a snort of bottled Alaska sunshine, that he had purchased in Juneau, to steady his nerves. This required him to take one hand off the thin rope, which was steadying him across the canyon. While tilting his head back to take his snort, he became unbalanced and almost before I realized it, lost his grip with his other hand on the rope and started to fall into the torrent below. Instinctively, I grabbed his free hand and wrapped my legs, strengthened by many hours of golf in Florida, around the log.

I had a firm grip on Grandpa Stoop's free hand. I told him to grab my other hand, which he refused to do until he had emptied his bottle of Alaska sunshine. When he was finished, he threw the empty bottle into the raging torrent below and grabbed my other hand. Using the strength gained from his libation, he easily swung himself back on the swaying log. He then quickly raised me to my feet beside him and we completed the rest of the crossing with no further difficulty.

Looking back across the canyon at, Tonto and Silverheels, we saw that the scorn on their faces had been replaced by fear. They indicated by Indian signs that they were afraid to cross the log bridge alone. Grandpa Stoops and I retraced our steps across the log bridge in order to help them cross.

Our journey to Rainbow Lake continued. Our difficulties were far from over. We still had miles of slippery rocks and roots, mud, the corduroy path, and tangled brush over which to travel. But suddenly, the beautiful log filled lake was before us.

While we rested, Tonto and Silverheels constructed a birch bark canoe in which they paddled us to the middle of the lake. We had no further mishaps except that Tonto and Silverheels each fell out of the canoe twice and had to be rescued by Grandpa Stoops and myself. The lake was swarming with hungry four-pound rainbow trout with which soon filled the canoe. Our dreams had been fulfilled.

Our return to Little Port Walters was somewhat less strenuous and eventful than our inland trip to Rainbow Lake because we were now going downhill. Learning from experience, we put blindfolds on Tonto and Silverheels when we came to Jake's Canyon and they were able to cross without the assistance of Grandpa Stoops or myself. We were slowed somewhat by the heavy load of rainbow trout we carried. However after several stumbles and falls and the pulling up of my rain pants, which continued to slip, we finally arrived back to where we had started that morning. We were met by Whiskers Brown, who flew us back to Juneau, where after several hours at the Red Dog Saloon, we no longer felt the pain of our cuts and bruises.

Cast Of Characters

(Grandpa Stoops) Reed Stoops II. Reed lived in Erie, Pennsylvania at the time of the story. He now lives in Florida during the winter season. He lives in Juneau during the summer.

(Tonto) Reed Stoops III. Reed has lived in Juneau for 28 years.

(Silverheels) Don Stoops. Don lived in Alaska at the time of this story. He now lives in Florida.

(Whiskers Brown) David Brown is a bush pilot.

(Jakes Canyon) Named for Jake Stoops son of Lee Stoops who has lived in Juneau for many years.

(Ray Theuret) Uncle and Great Uncle of the Stoops noted above. I have visited the Stoops in Juneau several times over the years.

Sergeant Kincaid's Last Gift

Completed November 5, 1996.

Sergeant Ralph Kincaid didn't want to go to Vietnam. He didn't want to leave his wife, Maria, and his two-year-old son, Ralph Jr. His son was an active child, never quiet, never staying in one place very long, always jumping around from one place to another, from one toy to another. He was, "just like a bee," his father laughed, "buzzing from one flower to another."

It was not long before he began calling him Buzzy and the name stuck, even after his father left for Vietnam.

Sergeant Kincaid hated to leave his wife and son. But he was a soldier and he did not complain or try to get his orders changed. He told his tearful wife Maria that she and Buzzy would be all right, that the year would soon pass and they would be back together again. The last thing he did before he left was to buy a beagle puppy for Buzzy. The boy was a little nervous when his father handed the puppy to him. But, the puppy licked his face and even before Sergeant Kincaid left for Vietnam, Buzzy and the puppy, which they named Sparky, became fast friends.

Sergeant Kincaid was only in Vietnam a month when he and a group of other soldiers were loaded into a helicopter and dropped off in the jungle to hunt for Vietcong. Two days later they were ambushed by a group of Vietcong and North Vietnamese and a fierce firefight took place. Gunships were called in and the Vietcong and North Vietnamese were eventually driven off, but not before most of the squad were wounded and several solders were killed including Sergeant Kincaid.

His body was shipped back to the States for burial. He was

entitled to be buried in Arlington, but Maria decided she wanted to have him buried in the little western Pennsylvania town, where they had grown up and where they had lived before he enlisted. The army sent a squad to the burial services and Sergeant Kincaid received a twenty-one gun salute and Maria received a folded American flag.

Maria and Buzzy received a small pension, but not nearly enough to live on. Maria got a job as a teller at the local bank and put Buzzy in a nursery school while she worked. She rented a small two-bedroom cottage and she and Buzzy began to get their lives back together. As the years passed, Maria never let Buzzy forget the connection between his father and his little dog, Sparky. Maria allowed Sparky to sleep beside the bed in Buzzy's room. Sometimes Buzzy would walk during the night and put his arm over the side of the bed so that Sparky could lick his hand. Reassured, Buzzy would soon fall asleep again.

And so the years passed and Buzzy was six-years-old, when Sparky went missing. Maria and Buzzy walked through their neighborhood looking for Sparky and calling his name. None of the neighbors had seen him. "Maybe he will come back by himself," Maria told Buzzy. But, he didn't.

A couple of nights later Maria heard Buzzy sobbing in his room after he had been put to bed. When she went into his room to comfort him, the six year old Buzzy wiped his eyes on his sleeve and cried. "Momma, where can Sparky be? He's been gone since last Thursday."

"I don't know," Maria replied. "He's always been a dependable dog and has never run off before. I've posted signs in the Post Office and the grocery store. We have no money to offer a reward. We'll have to wait and hope for the best."

Two days later Sparky was brought home by a young man

named, Harry Griswood, who lived on the other side of town. Harry was holding Sparky in his arms when Maria opened the door. "I saw your notice in the Post Office," Harry said. "Is this your dog?"

Buzzy was standing by the door with his mother. "Sparky!" he cried, as he took his dog from Harry's arms. Sparky wagged his tail and licked Buzzy's face obviously happy to be home.

"I guess he is," Harry said laughing. "I've had your dog for three days," he said. "I found him about five miles from town running along the road. He was limping so I stopped and picked him up. He had a sore paw, which has improved since I found him."

"How do you suppose he got so far from home?" Maria said.

"I don't know," Harry replied. "Although I've heard of a couple of similar cases lately. I suspect some not so bright kids are picking up dogs and taking them out in the country and dropping them off probably thinking the dogs will eventually find their way back home. Your dog was probably walking a couple of days before I picked him up. That's probably why he had a sore foot when I found him."

Harry had been a confirmed bachelor. A few days later, while in the bank, he asked Maria how the dog was. A week later, using the dog as an excuse, he talked to Maria at the bank again. This time he asked her to have dinner with him and she accepted.

Six months later, they were married. Maria had a new husband and Buzzy had a new father. Sergeant Kincaid's last gift had resulted in a replacement of himself.

Golf Ball

All Things In Some Manner Have Life (Spinoza)

Many think an inanimate object like me, a golf ball, has no
feelings or awareness of existence. They are wrong. Although
not made of flesh and blood, I too, when I was made, hoped for
a long and useful life. I hoped that I would obtain some special
distinction and would bring happiness wherever I went.

Made in the United States, I am proud to be American. I
and eleven others were placed in a colorful box and shipped to a
pro shop on a beautiful golf course. I hoped that whoever bought
me would be able to hit me high and long, down the middle of
the fairway. I dreamed that I would be bought by Arnold Palmer
or Jack Nicklaus or Tiger Woods. How marvelous it would be to
be sent high and far down the fairway with thousands cheering
my flight.

My dreams were not to be realized. My companions and
I were sold to a duffer who hit us everywhere, except down the
fairway. He selected me for his first shot of the day. He swung
wildly. He hit me into the woods. He didn't try to find me. "I
hit it too far to be able to find it," he said taking one of my box
companions and dropping it on the fairway. If the duffer had
taken the trouble to look for me he could have found me easily. I
had hit a limb of a tree and bounced back only two feet from the
fairway.

What a terrible day and night, I spent. I had landed in a
puddle and my beautiful white skin was covered with mud. A
rain that night buried me deeper in the ooze. After being hit only
once, I thought my career was over. I was in despair.

Then I heard a young woman's voice say, "I found a golf ball."

I could tell from her voice that she was young and beautiful. She plucked me out of the mud and wiped me clean. "Why, it's a brand new ball," she said. "I'll use it on the very next hole."

She cuddled me in her soft warm hand. I couldn't believe my good fortune. The hope I had once enjoyed again welled up in me. On the next tee she placed me on a brand new tee. I could sense her lining up carefully. I could hear the swish of her club. The next second I was flying high and straight down the fairway. What a glorious feeling!

I landed on the green and on the second bounce smacked into the flagstick and slid down into the cup. I heard my young lady shouting with excitement and her friends congratulating her. When she reached the green, my lady gingerly lifted me from the hole and kissed me.

My beautiful lady bought a pedestal for me and I now rest on her mantel. She always smiles at me and touches me for luck before she goes out to play golf. All the hopes and dreams I had when I was made have been realized.

[*Editor's note: This story was read at the author's memorial service by his granddaughter, April Leanne Walker.*]

The Bluebird of Happiness

This story was first read to the Bowie Senior Writers' Group in June 1997.

I am a Bluebird. My first conscious memory occurred just before I was born (hatched). Some look down on those that are hatched compared to the other method of birth. But, we are all God's creatures and equally valuable in his sight.

Just before I was born, I became vaguely aware that I was in a small dark enclosure. I felt somewhere within me a desperate urge to get out of the place that I was in. It seemed like a prison to me. I immediately began pecking at the walls that surrounded me. For some time, I could see no results from my pecking. I continued pecking, as my strength permitted, for the urge to be released was increasing with every peck. I heard other pecking sounds from nearby but I knew not what they were. At last, a tiny crack appeared in the wall that confined me. I directed my pecking at this crack and it gradually became wider. A light came in and momentarily blinded me. There had been no light in the enclosure I was in. I had been in a place of total darkness. The light increased my urge to be released and I continued pecking at the crack as hard and as fast as I could. At last the crack, before my now angry pecking, began to widen and then the walls collapsed entirely and I tumbled out into a totally new world. I was exhausted by my pecking and immediately closed my eyes and went to sleep.

I was awaked from my slumber by the fluttering of wings. I raised my head as high as my strength would allow and opened my beak as wide as I could. I did not do this by conscious thought. It was purely an instinctive reaction. A small brown

bird came in the hole in front of me and into the chamber that
I was in. She thrust her beak down my throat and I swallowed
a delicious grasshopper. The little brown bird immediately went
out the hole that she had entered. I had received several more
grasshoppers and beetles and other insects before I became aware
that this little brown bird with the dark blue on its wings and tail
was my mother.

I looked about me. I saw three other creatures in my chamber
that looked just like me. We were all in what I later learned was
called a nest, built of grass and small twigs. The nest had been
built up on the sides so that we wouldn't fall out. I again heard
the fluttering of wings. I raised my head and opened my beak
as wide as I could. But I was to be disappointed. The beetle this
bird had in his beak was thrust down the throat of one of the
other creatures in my nest. I learned later that he was my brother.
The other two creatures in my nest were my sisters. So, we were
an evenly divided family, two male and two female. We all had a
brother and we all had a sister.

The small bird that brought the beetle that fed my brother
had a bright blue back, a reddish breast and white belly. It turned
out that he was my father. All that day, the little brown bird
and the bird with the bright blue back took turns fluttering into
the hole to my chamber with grasshoppers and beetles or other
insects. I raised my head and opened my beak each time but was
fed only once in four times as was my brother and sisters. I and
my siblings were fed continuously until twilight that first day of
my life.

As twilight waned into darkness, I was aware of a soft
mellow warble, (purity, purity) outside the hole to my chamber.
My parents were singing their thanks for the joys of the day.

When my parents come north that spring, they had intended

to move into a small house made by humans. But a winter storm had blown this house off its pedestal and it was smashed when it hit the ground. The humans had not replaced it. When they found that the house they had lived in the prior year was no longer available, they immediately went house hunting. They searched for another house built by humans, but the only two they found had already been occupied by other birds. Finally, they found a hole in an old oak tree. The tree was at the edge of a woods. A large meadow spread out before it. The hole was twenty-five feet above the ground. The hole and the chamber behind it had been the former home of a woodpecker. The hole was larger than my parents would have liked. Its distance from the ground, my parents decided, provided adequate protection from predators and so they moved in. The chamber behind the hole had been hollowed out by the woodpecker until it was large enough for a roomy nest, which my parents immediately began to build out of grass and small sticks. It was in this home that my egg was laid and I was born.

The second day of my life was warm and sunny as had been on the day of my birth. I had no more than awakened from my night's slumber when I heard the flutter of wings and I immediately raised my head and opened my beak. The little brown bird, my mother, came in through the hole to our chamber. She put her beak deep into my throat and left a juicy beetle. She at once went out the hole and flew away. I had received the first meal of the day because my position in the nest was closest to the entrance to our chamber. The small bird with the blue back, my father, arrived at our nest soon after and fed my brother. Within a few moments, they both returned, first mother and then father, and my two sisters were fed. They continued to do this thoughout the day. I do not know how many grasshoppers, beetles and other insects I was fed that day, but my stomach was continually churning in order to digest the mass of food I was receiving.

My parents showed no preference to any one of us in the feedings we received. We each received share and share alike. The weather continued warm during the next few days. My parents took advantage of the weather and I and my siblings were continually fed. Always at the end of the day after the feedings stopped and as twilight turned into darkness I would hear the soft mellow warbling (purity purity) as my parents sang their thanks for the happiness of the day.

With all the food we were receiving we began to grow. By the end of the fourth day, I weighed twice as much as I had when I was born. I was changing in other ways than in size. When I was born, my body was completely naked. Now, I noticed the beginnings of the growth of feathers. They were little more than down at this stage but were the beginnings of feathers nevertheless. My beak was larger and I no longer needed to struggle to raise my head at feedings. Regardless of my larger size and new strenth, I received the same amount of food, as my parents continued to feed us all equally.

At the end of the first week of my life, the weather changed. It became cold and on looking out of the entrance of my nest, I could see rain falling. At the change in the weather, our feedings stopped for awhile. My mother came into the nest and spread her wings and body over us. We were soon as warm as toast. The rain increased and the wind began to blow and before long was howling around our tree. Our tree began bending and twisting as the gale increased in intensity. I could feel the movement of the tree as I lay warm and safe under my mother. I knew I would have been frightened if she had not been there. My father perched himself at the entrance to our nest and thereby prevented the rain from coming in.

Warm and dry under my mother, the gentle sway of the tree lulled me to sleep. When I awoke, the storm had passed. Looking out of the entrance to our nest, I could see that the rain had stopped and that the sun was shining. At the end of the storm, my mother had left the nest. She had gone to find food for us. Because of the rain and because evening was near, it was difficult to find food and so my siblings and I received only one meal that day. As always as twilight turned into darkness, I could hear "purity, purity," as my parents sang of the joys of the day and because their little ones were safe. During the time, I lived in our nest we had several storms. Always my mother would come into our nest and spread her wings and warm body over us.

When we were two weeks old, we had a bad fright. A cat came to our neighborhood and started to climb our tree. I was the first to see him as I was looking out the entrance to our nest. I saw that he was too big to get through the entrance to our nest. But I thought that he might be able to stick his paw though the entrance and grab us in his claws and drag us out. I pushed my siblings to the very back of the nest. Fortunately, our home had been constructed by a much larger bird than a bluebird and thus was deeper in the tree than it would have been if constructed by a bird our size. In addition, my parents had built our nest in the rear of our chamber. These factors gave me some hope that we would not come to harm; nevertheless, I was badly frightened.

The cat was only partly up the tree when my mother, returning from her food gathering, spotted the cat. She sent out a call 'oola, oola' for help and my father was there in seconds. They started dive-bombing the cat. They came at him from all directions giving a good peck with each dive. When I became aware that my parents were on the job, I got enough courage to look outside again. The cat was about ten feet off the ground. He was clinging to the tree with his back claws and one front paw. It might have been comical if it hadn't been so serious. As my parents came at him, he would swipe at them with his free paw. He never came close to snagging them for they were much too fast for him. When my parents came at him from different directions at the same time he loosened the hold of his other front paw on the tree in order to take a swipe at both my parents. He lost his grip and tumbled to the ground. He had had enough. He took one more look at the entrance to our nest twenty-five feet above and then started to run to his house in the distance. My parents encouraged his decision by continuing to dive-bomb him until he was well out of our area. That evening, as twilight turned into night, the song of my parents contained a special note of thankfulness.

Two and a half weeks had now passed since our birth. We all had feathers. They were not full-grown but they were feathers. We were beginning to move around the nest. I was not always now the one nearest to the hole in our tree. I was not the only one who looked out the hole. On our seventeenth day birthday, one of my sisters edged her way to the hole and looked out. Hoping to see better, she climbed up to the hole and perched where she had seen our mother and father perch. A sudden gust of wind unbalanced her and she fell. We all were horrified. My sister fluttered her wings as she had seen our parents do but to no avail. While she had feathers, they were not sufficiently grown for her to fly. They did however soften her fall to the ground. As a result, she was not injured by her fall. My parents were soon there but there was nothing they could do.

A few moments after my sister's fall, a human came near

our tree. He saw my sister on the ground. He picked her up and examined her. He saw that she had not been injured. He looked up at the hole twenty-five feet from the ground.

"We will have to get you back to your nest," he said. Cupping my sister in his two hands he started walking to the human house in the distance. We thought that this was the last we would ever see of our sister. He will probably feed her to "that cat" we moaned. However in a few minutes we saw him returning. He was carrying my sister in a small box. He also was carrying a long ladder. He placed the ladder against the tree and with the box containing my sister climbed the ladder to the entrance of our nest. He gently removed my sister from the box and placed her in the nest with the rest of us.

"Be careful little one and don't fall out of your nest again," he said. "Grow up to be a beautiful bluebird."

We, her brothers and sister, were overjoyed at her return. My parents' song that evening as twilight turned to darkness contained an extra note of thankfulness.

And so the days passed. We were now full-feathered bluebirds and as large as our parents. Our home in the oak tree was getting very crowded. We knew that the time was quickly coming when we would have to leave our cozy home and go out into the world on our own. We had mixed feelings about leaving our home. We compared the security we were receiving from our parents with the satisfaction of gaining independence. And, we were afraid. We remembered our sister who had fallen out of our nest and was helpless on the ground. What if our wings were not strong enough to support us in flight and we ended up on the ground as she had done? Once out of the nest, who would feed us? How would we find food? But our parents became ever more insistent that we leave. They knew that the time had come when the care they had provided must end. They stopped bringing food to our nest. They flew out of our nest and back several times to show us how to fly. They tried to impart to us (to paraphrase Robert Louis Stevenson) their joy of flying up in the air and up in the sky so blue. They said it was the most joyous thing that a bluebird could do.

Finally, the time came when I could no longer resist my parents' insistence that I leave. I stood at the entrance to our home. My feet grasped the edge of the hole. I swayed back and forth and looked down at the ground. It seemed so far away. I was thinking that perhaps I should return to my nest and leave some other time, when I received a gentle push from my mother. I fell away from the hole. I started flapping my wings as fast as I could. I flew up into a nearby tree. My wings were strong from the many grasshoppers, beetles and other insects my parents had provided for me since my birth so many days ago. I looked about me. On a nearby limb, a beetle slowly crawled. I had my first meal after I left home.

Yesterday, I met a blue bird that looks a lot like my mother. I saw her first in the tree next to mine. When I called, "Oola, oola," she replied and I flew over to her tree. We have agreed to fly south together to a warmer climate when fall arrives and it turns cold. We will return together in the spring and to find a home and start a family of our own. Truly, I have become a bluebird of happiness.

[Author's note: I received the idea for this story from a sermon by Rev. Richard Stetler, St. Matthew's United Methodist Church. The sermon was delivered on May 11, 1997 and was entitled "Where is your nest?"]

A Second Life

I had not expected to die so soon. Although up in years, I was in apparently good health. A recently completed examination by my doctor had revealed no serious physical problems.
But, here I was. I felt light and airy. I felt blissful and serene. Although I did not know where I was, I felt no fear. I had no desire to return to the place that I had left.

Almost immediately, there appeared before me what I at first thought was an apparition but quickly realized was a person like myself. "Where am I and who are you?" I asked. I realized that my voice was not accusatory or harsh as it might have been in the place from where I had come.

"Some from your world call this heaven and some call it paradise. Others call it by different names. Here, we have no name for this place. It is just the principal place of existence. Unlike the place where you came from, which is temporary, this place has existed forever and will continue to exist forever."

"Where, in what I knew as the universe, is this place. How large is it?"

"You are in about the same location in the universe as the place you came from but in a different dimension. This place goes on forever in every direction. It has no borders."

"I am an old man and I knew I was not long for the world. But I was in good physical health. I did not expect to come here quite so soon. What happened?"

"You stepped in front of a truck."

"Oh-Oh. I remember nothing."

"You were killed instantly."

"Are you Saint Peter?"

"No. I have just been assigned to get you started in your

new existence. Peter shares this duty with millions of others. We all take our turn. Thousands a day arrive here. All are assigned somebody like me to assist them on arrival. Peter was a good man and upon his death received immediate admission to this place. But when he arrived, there were already hundreds of millions here. Most of the people who had lived since creation preceded him here."

"What did you say your name was?"

"I didn't say but my name is Harold. I came here in 1066 as recorded in your time. I was killed in the Battle of Hastings."

"Then you are a king?"

"Was a king. No kings here. Here everybody is the same. Everybody is equal. Having obtained prominence in your previous existence means nothing here."

"You said that Peter was a good man and received immediate admission here. Does that mean that some are not so fortunate and are sent to the lake of fire that preachers threaten the people with back where I came from?"

"There is no such place. What kind of monster do such people think God is? God gets very angry with those who say that he punishes by eternal torture those he gave freedom of choice when he created them and who act different that he would have liked them to do. None of these preachers are granted immediate entrance to this place. Some wait years and a few wait millenniums for admission."

"You perhaps remember the prophet Samuel who drove King Saul mad and who said that God wanted all the Amalekites killed, including women, children, and even the cattle. Samuel made God so angry by this assertion that, although 3000 years have passed, he hasn't yet gained entrance to this place."

"Where are Samuel and the others who have not gained

admission to this place? Are there many?"

"They are in a different dimension than we are in, a place of contemplation and rebirth. From this dimension, unlike the earth, they can look directly into this place but are not allowed to enter until their natures have completely changed. It is impossible to fake such a change. God cannot be fooled."

"Compared to the total number people who have lived on Earth, there are comparably fewer people in this place of rebirth, perhaps two million at the present time. Most are recent arrivals. A few will be released in as little as a week. But most take much longer. Human nature does not change that easily. A few individuals, like Samuel, have been there for centuries. These people are not being punished except by the memory of their misdeeds on Earth, the fact that they have not been admitted here and have to associate with people like themselves."

"How did I escape this place of rebirth. I was far from perfect. I lost my temper many times. I sassed my mother when I was young, didn't appreciate how hard my father worked until it was too late to tell him, got mad occasionally at my brother, and didn't help my sisters like I should have. I didn't always tell the truth. While I loved my wife and children, I at times was more concerned with the progress of my career than with them. I wasn't always as generous as I should have been. While I was born poor, I had it pretty nice most of my life. I always had a lot of great friends. At the time, I didn't appreciate this as I should have. I am surprised that I don't have to spend some time, perhaps a long time, in the rebirth dimension."

"Well, you were a borderline case. What saved you was that when you did something or acted in a way you shouldn't have, you felt bad about it and wished you had acted differently. When you didn't tell the truth it was generally because you were fearful of what the truth would reveal about yourself or others. We have no record of you lying in order to hurt somebody else."

"No, I don't think I ever did that. At least, I hope not."

"You were at times a little too ambitious but it was generally because you wanted to make the most of the gifts you were born with and because you wanted to bring security to those you loved."

"Well, I wouldn't give myself as high a rating but I am happy that you think so here."

"Shall we get going? I am sure you will have many more questions as we proceed."

Pit Hole

This is the first chapter of an unfinished novel.

I was born late one night shortly after the turn of the Century. The bleak farm house in which I was born, although older, looked little different than it had sixty years before Great-Grandfather Ben had arrived in the house with his new bride. The same dusty road in summer is quagmired in spring by the winter's melting snow still winds its way wearily past its unpainted doors and now tumbles down porches. The same gray smoke that comes from the chestnut blocks burning in the cast iron stoves curls slowly from the chimney moss covered by the passing years. The stately maples sheltering the house from the summer sun and blending with the countryside emblazons the glory of autumn.

My countryside had begun to decay. The prosperity, which had followed the years after the Civil War, was beginning to ebb away. The large farms, which the pioneers had partly cleared in the early 18th century, had by 1870 been divided among his numerous off spring into compact farms of 60 to 100 acres. The opening, after the War, of the oil boomtowns of Oil City, Titusville, Petroleum Center, Franklin and Pit hole gave the country people an abundant market for their produce. The early struggles of the previous generation were past and for the next 30 years this countryside was to prosper as few lands had ever before. Its prosperity would continue until the decay of the boom towns took away the markets and the automobiles. The high wages of the city took away the young people. Their departure left the countryside lonely, many of the still fertile fields untilled and houses decayed and empty, a habitat of bats and mice.

They would fall almost unnoticed among the weeds and second growth.

In the year in which I was born, the decay had already started. The final surge of the Great War would furnish the final blow to undo her. It could not in truth be said that the countryside died and was deserted because except for the few unworked farms and deserted houses, she appeared the same. The older people stayed on and still lived much as they had in the past. But, the young had left and the rest of the country had grown past her. There were not many who mourned her passing or even knew or cared that she was dead. There were some, however, who sensed the loss and who wished for the good old days of her ascendancy to return.

Looking back on her now, we see that her prejudices were strong, sometimes cruel. Her superstitions many, sometimes to foolishness but her kindness was all embracing, her prosperity was real, and her way of life gave a security unlikely ever to return to this generation.

As a lad wandering over the still tilled fields and through the remaining woodlands, my feet often carried me to an old deserted house nestled among some second growth. Although now decayed by lack of use, it could be seen that in the past, by her size and beauty, it had undoubtedly been a place of pride and show about the countryside. Often as I wandered through her deserted rooms, I wondered what tales she could tell if given a tongue to speak. Tales of the loves, the jealousies, the hates, the fears, the joys, the kindness her walls had sheltered. Often as I climbed her still sturdy stairs or gazed from her broken windows, I imagined I could hear the laughter of those her doors had protected. Then again on cloudy days, I imagined I could hear shouts and curses faintly. But most often, I could hear the tinkle of laughter ringing to my ears, the gay laughter of maid and laddie happy in their love, the silvery shouts of children racing though her halls, the coarse laughter of men at their cups, and the soft laughter of women secure at their baskets.

[Author's Note: This is the first chapter of my novel "Pit hole." It will probably be the last. It would require a lot of research to write, which I am in no position to do. Pit hole is located about 5 miles from Titusville. It was an oil boomtown during the 1870s. It had opera houses and whorehouses at the time, just like the western old gold or silver boomtowns, everything a boomtown needs. Nothing remains there today.]

Part Three: *Poetry*

Ray with his wife Alice shortly after their wedding.

In the spring before he died, he looked across the dining room table at his wife of 66 years. He turned to his daughter and said, "Look at her. She is as beautiful as the day I married her."

Spring

The April rains arrive
The winter meadow
Turns lush and green
For spring is here

The larks return
And in the sky
Sing their low sweet song
For spring is here.

The daffodils bright yellow heads
Have left the earth
And wave in the mellow breeze
For spring is here.

I leave my winter abode
And return to home and friends
And meadows, larks and daffodils
For spring is here.

Tragedy At Age Seven

I see big cousin fishing in brook.
I get and bend pin. Get string and stick.
I put worm on pin. Drop in brook.
The line yanks. I lift pin and fish out of water.
I stand frozen as I see the fish wiggle and wiggle
It falls back into the brook.
Tragedy

The Return Of The Snowbird

The April rains arrive
The winter meadow
Turns lush and green
For spring is here

The larks return
And in the sky
Sing their low sweet song
For spring is here

The daffodils bright yellow heads
Have left the earth
And wave in the mellow breeze
For spring is here

I leave my winter abode
And return to home and friends
And meadows, larks and daffodils
For spring is here

Part Four: *Tributes*

Ray and Alice Theuret were friends with Joe and Mary Morello throughout their lives. Here they are together on one of their many outings.

In Memoriam of Ray Theuret

By Lee Stoops on Behalf of the Stoops Family

Over the final decade of his wonderful life, our Uncle
Ray became a wordsmith. Knowing how much he would
enjoy it, we are going to craft our own new word to describe a
man that injected nothing but joy into the lives of each of us.
BEAUTACIOUS is that word. He was as beautiful and gracious
a person as we have ever known – and that was in spite of the
fact that he was related to we, Stoops'.

When a person we love departs our world, he or she
normally leaves us with just memories of our time together.
Uncle Ray left us much more than that. He took the time and
effort to leave us a record of special remembrances from his own
life. He spent much of the last decade writing down many of the
anecdotes and stories of his past that undoubtedly helped shape
him into the beautacious man that we all knew.

While I rarely had the pleasure of seeing Uncle Ray more
than once a year during my life, it was always a highlight of the
year. In Alaska, however, I did have the honor of assisting him
with the editing of many of his life stories. In reading about
the events and relationships that he chose to remember as
meaningful, I felt like I came to know him better than almost
any person I have ever known. Again, beautacious comes to
mind. His significant memories are stories that seem simple on
the surface, but invariably have a theme of triumph over adversity
and the display of virtue. If you wish to pay special tribute to
the passing of this great friend, please take the time to read the
stories he wanted to share. You will know him and appreciate
him even more than you do today. He left us his memories so

that we could share in their warmth.

The Stoops family has far more than just warm memories of our Uncle Ray, we have ONLY warm memories. On the golf course of life, every round we played with Uncle Ray was under the brightest sun. There was never a need to keep score, because we have always been winners just for knowing him.

Our hearts are with the Theuret family today, while our heads are tilted upward to salute our departed friend. And, one more time, Uncle Ray, our special words: "We love you, man!"

[Editor's Note: Lee Stoops was Ray Theuret's great-nephew, son of his niece by marriage, Norma Strict Stoops, who is the daughter of Marie Akerly Strict, his wife Alice's sister and his sister-in-law. Lee lives in Alaska but visited Florida frequently and visited Ray at those times. Lee Stoops is also a writer and was one of the people Ray shared his writing with. He was very fond of Lee and thought of him as he would a son.]

Tribute in Memory of Ray Morse Theuret

By Gordon Harvey delivered June 7, 2004 at the Memorial Service

Ray was a work colleague but more importantly he was my friend. I first met him in the early 1960's. He was my District Manager and I was an intern in a newly created regional office in Baltimore. We later worked together at our Agency's headquarters where Ray was a Director. We worked for the US Army Audit Agency, a wonderful worldwide organization that contributed greatly to our lives and careers. We traveled extensively and our lives were enriched by the diversity of the world's various cultures. Our travels broadened the borders of our limited understanding. The camaraderie that developed among the people in the Agency followed us throughout our lifetimes. It was an unusual, unexplainable, special bond that could not be broken. Once you became an Army Auditor, you were always an Army Auditor. An Army Audit Alumni Organization exists today and meets regularly. Some of its members are here today.

Ray was very helpful to me in my early career. He retired, however, a few years after we first met. In the early days, I learned how to precisely replicate Ray's distinctive initial that he used to approve official documents. His initial looked like an inverted "V" crossed by a mark that resembled a portion of a safety pin. Much later, I showed Ray how I could replicate his infamous "T", which, of course, stood for Theuret. Jokingly, I told him I probably approved some of my own promotions along the way and perhaps a few special trips.

I got to know Ray much better after he and Alice moved to Bowie and began attending St. Matthew's. We played golf together. And, sometimes some of our Army Audit friends joined us. When Ray was 88 years old, he beat me at golf. Some who know how I play golf will not be impressed—but I was. He shot his age in golf when he was 81. Ray was energetic and very involved throughout his long life. As recent as a couple of years ago, he would surprise us by moving quickly from the golf cart to retrieve a lost ball before its owner could get to it. His golf shots were almost always straight down the fairway and in bounds.

And, that is the way he lived his life—always straight and in bounds. Although we were separated by almost 30 years in age, he and I had a lot in common. For example, we shared a common background. We were farm boys. Material things did not enrich our earlier days. Our faith journey was similar. We attended the First Church of God whose headquarters is in Anderson, Indiana. The fundamentalist principles taught in this church environment always provided a special guidance in our lives. Both of us were proud of our heritage. Ultimately, we both ended up at St. Matthew's in Bowie—far from our Pennsylvania and West Virginia roots.

Bowie provided us an opportunity for many exchanges about religion and other aspects of life. We often talked of our faith journey and its meaning to us. We both recognized that without some doubts faith cannot exist. To some degree Ray bought into my simple explanation of my faith that comes from the old spiritual hymn *We Will Understand It Better By and By.* We last spoke about his faith journey just a few days ago, when I visited him in the Rehabilitation Center in Annapolis. Ray told me he was ready to go to his heavenly home and was eager to get there.

But, Ray's influence on my life transcended religion and our work life. He touched my life in another way. He knew that sometime ago our federal government had falsely, unjustly, and illegally prosecuted me. It was a political prosecution that lasted for over four years. Ray became fascinated with this story and probed me for more details almost every time we spoke. Over time, he got to know a great deal about my story. He knew, for example, it was a story about political corruption by political zealots and the evil that sometimes envelops our political process. But, more importantly, Ray saw more to the story. Ray was a writer and he knew that, although I was completely exonerated by a federal appeals court, I was still reluctant to follow his often-repeated advice to write my story. He considered my story a St. Matthew's story—a part of my faith journey. He saw it as a story of integrity and ethics, of moral courage and courageous risks, of family, of God working in mysterious ways, of a miracle, of forgiveness and recovery, and of equal importance, a story of hope—a ripple of hope for our nation.

So, one day about 18 months ago while golfing, I told Ray a poignant story related to my prosecution that I had not revealed to him or to anyone else—it was a beautiful experience that occurred here at St. Matthew's—in this sanctuary—very early on a summer morning. After hearing this story, Ray had had enough of my vacillating. As directly as he could, he said to me, Gordon you must write your story. The story was covered-up by the political side of our government and you need to tell it. Your grand children will want to know. Your grandchildren need to know. The story has lessons that will guide them in their life's journey. Your verbal renditions will not last. You must write it! I began to write my story the following week.

When I saw Ray a few days ago for our last visit, I told him I had just completed my book. Although he was feeling very poorly, his radiant, approving smile said more than any comment he could have made. I plan to dedicate my book in Ray's memory.

In closing, I would like to recite a writing entitled "The

Ship," written by Henry Scott Holland, that is most appropriate for Ray's passing:

Death

I am standing on the seashore.
A ship spreads her white sails to the
    morning breeze and starts for the ocean.
I stand watching her until she fades on the
    horizon,
and someone at my side says,
"She is gone."

Gone where?

The loss of sight is in me, not in her.
Just at the moment when someone says,
"She is gone,"
there are others who are watching her
    coming.
Other voices take up the glad shout,
"Here she comes,"
and that is dying.